THE CYCLE

**JOHN
WAYNE
COMUNALE**

Grindhouse Press
PO BOX 521
Dayton, Ohio 45401

Grindhouse Press #057
ISBN-10: 1-941918-52-2
ISBN-13: 978-1-941918-52-4

This is a work of fiction. All characters and events portrayed in this book are fictitious and any resemblance to real people or events is purely coincidental.

Other titles by John Wayne Comunale

For Chaos.
There are no rules.

"I GUESS IT'S NOT TOO spooky," Beth said out loud to no one.

She stood next to her old black Jeep, looking up the winding gravel driveway at the house it led to. Her Jeep wasn't the kind that the doors and top came off because it was a four-door Cherokee edition. She didn't drive it because she was the kind of person who went off-roading or on excursions into the wilderness. Like most things Beth owned, the vehicle was a hand-me-down, and in a sense, so was the small house up the hill at the end of the driveway.

She had inherited it. Actually, her mother inherited it when her sister, Agnes, died three weeks ago but wanted nothing to do with it and signed the house over to her daughter. In doing so she hoped to spur Beth on to independence while remaining close enough to home to keep an eye on.

Beth didn't truly know her aunt but remembered meeting her once when Agnes showed up to her sixth birthday party. Spring was ending and it was warm outside but not hot yet, so Beth's mother decided to have the party in a neighborhood park. A woman approached Beth as she walked back to the picnic tables from a field where she had been playing kickball with the other kids. The stranger stepped from the trees, seemingly from nowhere, and blocked Beth's path.

"Hello, Beth," she said, smiling down at the girl.

Beth stopped and used her hand to block the sun from her eyes to better see the odd-looking woman. She thought it might be one of her friend's mother's, but Beth didn't recognize her. The woman was dressed so differently and stood out amongst the other moms, but Beth didn't remember seeing her until just then. Her mother was wearing white tennis shoes, knee-length shorts, and a sleeveless polo shirt. The other moms wore something similar, but the woman standing in front of Beth had on a black skirt down to her ankles despite the warm weather.

She also wore a modest peasant-style blouse adorned with a broach of polished stone above her heart. The stone was marked with a funny symbol that looked similar to a heart but not quite. The smell of what Beth would come to know later as sage and patchouli rolled off the woman in soft, fragrant waves.

Her hair was dark and straight like Beth's mother but much longer and pulled back so the true length was hidden behind her neck. The woman bore a striking resemblance to Beth's mother in the face, but the odd clothes and long hair distracted from it.

"I'm your Aunt Agnes," the woman continued.

Before Beth could reply she heard her mother calling from across the park.

"Beth! I said get over here this instant!" She was stomping across the field toward them.

"Go on," Aunt Agnes said with a light smile. "You shouldn't keep your mother waiting."

Her mother caught Beth by the arm and yanked the girl away from the woman claiming to be her aunt.

"What did I tell you about talking to her? It's far too early for this!"

Beth's mother stepped between them and continued her angry rant in a hushed tone. She could no longer hear exactly what her mother was saying but could tell from the rapid-fire delivery and inflection the two weren't happily reminiscing about days gone by. Beth did manage to catch a few words here and there, but without context they meant nothing to her.

The words *age, plan, interfere,* and *cycle* barely registered with the confused young girl who was still trying to figure out why her mom was so angry at this strange woman. Beth looked over to the picnic table where her friends were gathered, intently watching the incident unfurl just as she was.

When she looked back her mother was standing over at the space in the trees Aunt Agnes had stepped out from. She turned around and walked back over to Beth but was now alone.

"Don't worry about that." She kneeled in front of her daughter and brushed the wind-swept hair from her eyes. "Mother took care of it. Now, do you know what time it is?"

Beth was stunned and silent. She didn't understand anything about what had happened, and her young brain ached trying to make sense of it. All she could do was stare into her mother's eyes, hoping an answer would appear within the deep, gray pools, but Beth saw only her reflection.

"It's time to open presents!"

Just like that Beth snapped out of it, and nothing in the world mattered more than opening presents. She never gave the incident another thought.

BETH NEVER HEARD ANYTHING ELSE of Aunt Agnes
until a few weeks ago when she'd died, and a lawyer came to the
house to let them know. He claimed to have been trying to contact
Beth's mother by phone and registered mail, but his attempts had
been ignored. She acted as if she couldn't care less that her sister
died and said as much to the lawyer.

When he told Beth's mother Aunt Agnes had left her the house
she roundly refused and told the man to give it away to a charity or
burn it down. Either way she wanted nothing to do with her sister's
house or, as she called it, 'that dusty shit-hole out in the woods'.
Beth glanced at the address on the paperwork and saw her aunt had
lived on the edge of town in a wooded area at the base of the mountain.

The lawyer told them Aunt Agnes had a stipulation in her will
that the house remain in the family and could not be handed off or
sold to a non-relative.

"What if I took it over, Mom?"

Beth said the words at the exact same time she was thinking
them with little to no delay between. Her mother shot a look at

4

Beth she'd never seen aimed her way. A look reserved more for those who'd hurt her. Beth had no idea why, but for some reason what she'd said had been tantamount to betrayal in her mother's eyes.

"Well, that would be the next easiest thing to do seeing as I'm already here," the lawyer said, oblivious of the unspoken exchange between the two women. "I assume you're over eighteen, yes?"

"I'm twenty-three actually," Beth spouted quickly, although her voice softened toward the end.

"If your mother agrees," he continued while shuffling some of the many papers he'd spread across the kitchen table, "I can hand ownership of the house over to you immediately."

Beth swung her gaze back to her mother, whose expression now refashioned itself to silently scream anger. The fact of the matter was Beth wanted to move out, and quite frankly her mother wanted it as well. It wasn't that Beth was a bad kid, she'd just never lived away from home, and her mother thought it was time she gain some independence and learn what it's like out in the real world.

They'd had several conversations about it over the past few months, weighing pros and cons while trying to formulate a plan for Beth they could both agree on. Having a free house dropped in their lap sounded like it could be a big part of that plan.

She wasn't going to school at the moment, which was another reason her mother wanted her to move out. She didn't particularly care if Beth went to college or not. Her mother wanted to remove the safety net of home so Beth could figure out what she wanted to do while getting a dose of reality.

Beth could tell her mother did not agree by the way she sneered and drummed her fingers against the table. The house had to stay in the family, and Beth moving into it for free would mean her mother wouldn't have to pay half the rent on an apartment for the first six months, which was something they'd agreed upon during one of their many discussions.

"Fine," her mother finally said through clenched teeth, breaking the few tense seconds of silence. "Move into the damn house. Live their forever for all I care."

Beth's mother reached across the table, snatched the document from the lawyer's hand, and attacked the paper with inky scratches in the shape of her name. Now, here Beth was two weeks later, looking up the driveway at a house she still couldn't believe was actually hers, terrified to take another step.

The house wasn't scary once Beth got up close. It was actually quaint and much less intimidating than it appeared from the end of the driveway. From that distance it had seemed to loom large with an underlying sinister quality peeking out from between the cracks. The things her mother had to say, or rather the lack thereof, about Aunt Agnes didn't help assuage Beth's nervousness.

On the drive over she was more excited than she could ever remember being about anything in her life so far, but now that she was standing at the door, her door, key in hand, the excitement changed to an icy fear. Beth wasn't afraid because the house was creepy. She was afraid of what the house represented, which was her independence. This was her first time living away from home, and she wanted to be able to show her mother and herself she was able to handle the responsibility.

The key was on a ring by itself, which she'd put around her middle finger where it dangled from a hand she couldn't stop from shaking.

"Jesus, Beth, get it together," she said out loud to herself, hoping the sound of her own voice would calm her enough to see how ridiculous it was to be afraid.

The door felt sturdy despite the cosmetic wear to the faded red paint that chipped and flaked in areas where the sun had been particularly brutal. Beth thought it looked slightly wider than the front door of a house was supposed to be but decided it was the frame that made it appear that way. She knew she was stalling taking in these details, but she did make a mental note to measure the width of the door later to see if she was correct.

There was a single deadbolt lock above an old steel doorknob that predated the kind of modern knobs with a locking mechanism built in. Beth raised the key, slid it in the narrow space on the deadbolt, and heard the familiar click of turning tumblers. That couldn't be right, though, because she hadn't turned the key yet. Beth pulled her hand back quick, like it had shocked her. She was sure she'd heard it, hadn't she?

She stared at the key, trying to decide whether to reach for the doorknob or turn around and drive back home.

"No," Beth said. "I'm imagining things because Mother put them in my head. This is home now. This is *my* home."

Before she could talk herself out of it Beth reached for the knob, turned it, and pushed against the door, but it didn't budge. It was still locked. Relieved but feeling foolish, Beth now knew she'd imagined hearing the lock turn on its own. It was probably a twig snapping from the branch of one of the many trees surrounding the property as a squirrel hurriedly climbed its way to an easy meal.

Beth reached for the key, grabbed it between her thumb and forefinger, and slowly turned. This time she was positive the tumblers engaged and absolutely sure she heard the click signifying so. She dropped her hand to the doorknob but paused and looked over her shoulder before trying to open the door again.

The Jeep was close behind, and a soft voice whispered in her head to turn around and run, but she quickly shook away the thought. She turned back around to face the peeling red ingress, threw her hand at the knob, and opened the door.

THREE

BETH STOOD OVER A SINK full of soapy water, running a sponge across one of the two plates she'd brought with her. The lawyer told Beth and her mother the house included some furniture along with various other household items, but as far as she was concerned the place was fully furnished. There were cups and plates in the kitchen cabinets far nicer and of better quality than the two plates she bought at the dollar store.

Just a few hours earlier Beth was almost too scared to enter the home, and now she didn't want to leave. The outside of the house was weathered and worn, but inside was an entirely different story. The place was neatly kempt and clean and still felt lived in despite having not been for several weeks. It was almost like Beth was only housesitting while her Aunt went away on a permanent vacation.

When she walked through the door she was hit with the familiar aroma of Aunt Agnes, and all her imagined fears dissolved into the scent. Beth felt at ease and suddenly couldn't remember what she had been so scared of in the first place?

The front door opened to a small living room with a brown couch at the center of the wall and a matching high-backed chair and ottoman to the left of it. The floors were hardwood, but there was a round area rug laid out in front of the three pieces of furniture. A fireplace was across the room at the center of the wall with a sad and empty log-holder sitting off to the side. To the right of the unfortunately colored couch was a hallway leading to the rest of the house.

The single room on the right looked like Aunt Agnes used it as a study or personal library. An antique writing desk sat against the wall to the right, but every other inch of wall space in the room was occupied by overflowing bookshelves. Across the hall was the master bedroom with a bathroom, the only bathroom in the house, attached. An ornately carved four-poster bed dominated the room along with a five-drawer dresser that came up to Beth's chest.

The hall ended at the quaint and cozy kitchen where Beth discovered the bounty of vintage dishes. She stood at the sink, absently rewashing the same dish while staring out the window at the trees lining the far edge of the backyard. The setting sun dipped below the highest branches, and the forest's shadow spread quickly across the yard, blotting out the light. The sudden change snapped Beth from her daze, and she shook her head, chuckling.

"All this moving must have taken it out of me," she said. "I was really zoned out there for a second."

Beth removed the plate from the soapy water, ran it under the faucet, and placed it in the drying rack next to its mate. She knew she should eat something soon but wanted to sit and relax for a while first. Beth felt like she hadn't stopped moving since she walked through the door, which was pretty much true. Despite not having a lot to actually move in, she was meticulous with each item and took her time.

There wasn't a T.V. in the house, and her mother wouldn't allow her to bring the one from her room at home, so relaxing to garbage programming was out of the question. Another thing her mother kept was Beth's cellphone, citing it was *her* phone because she paid for it. If Beth were no longer living at home she'd have to obtain and pay for her own phone.

It wasn't a complete surprise since getting her own phone was one of the issues they discussed and agreed on during earlier conversations they'd had about her moving out. Since the move was so sudden Beth wasn't able to take the steps necessary to procure a phone, the most important of those steps being to save the money needed to buy one. It was high on the list of her priorities though.

Beth remembered the tremendous amount of books in the study and turned to head that way after she pulled the plug in the sink.

"I hope Aunt Agnes had good taste in books."

The last of the dishwater sucked through the drain and gurgled down into the pipes as Beth left the kitchen, passing by the one door in the house she hadn't opened yet.

The basement door.

BETH WAS AWARE OF THE basement door but chose to ignore it. She passed by it a dozen times while bringing armfuls of her belongings in from the Jeep. She didn't have a lot of things to move so the kitchen was the perfect size to act as a staging area, and she stacked boxes on and next to the small round table.

After bringing in the first few boxes Beth had lingered in front of the basement door, vacillating between exploring the space now or after she'd unpacked. Her back spasmed with an involuntary shiver, and she decided to investigate after she'd moved her stuff in and had some time to acclimate to her new home. The unease she'd felt before entering the house was freshly dissipated, and she didn't want to stir it back up right away.

She had never been afraid of the dark, nor had the sight of spiders, roaches, or rats ever elicited even a modicum of fear in her. This was one of the ways Beth was different from the girls she'd been friends with growing up. She never understood what it was about those things that made the other kids squirm and shriek so unnecessarily.

The idea struck Beth as a cheesy cliché, and she wondered if her friends really were afraid of creepy crawly things or just thought they were supposed to be. Had they been conditioned to react this way after witnessing their mothers exhibit the behavior? Did they realize their fear was based on nothing but the distant echo of a stranger's reaction?

Beth remembered being four years old and sitting on a stool in the kitchen watching her mother cut chicken breasts on the counter for dinner. A three-inch, fat brown tree roach appeared from under the toaster and made a dash across the counter toward the slimy, raw meat. Beth's mother saw it from the corner of her eye, and the hand she wasn't holding the knife in shot over and scooped up the roach.

She held it up by its head between her thumb and forefinger while six legs flailed as the pest twisted its thorax trying to escape. The struggling stopped a second later when her mother crushed the roach's head with a crunchy, wet pop. She dropped the carcass to the floor, wiped her fingers on her apron, and went back to cutting the chicken.

"You've got to crush their heads, dear," her mother said, glancing up at Beth for a moment. "Otherwise they don't die all the way."

Since then Beth had killed many cockroaches in the same manner, much to the chagrin of any mixed company she happened to be in. There would most likely be roaches in the basement, although she couldn't imagine many with as clean and tidy as Aunt Agnes had kept her house. There would be spiders for sure though. They came standard issue with basements no matter how clean you kept things.

The dwindling sunlight made the study dark, and Beth pulled the short chain on the small lamp at the corner of the desk. With the light on Beth could see the books lined against the back of the desk were actually journals, a lot of journals.

These weren't cheap, mass-produced ones found perpetually on sale at Hallmark. The journals she was looking at were clearly custom made and most likely hand-fashioned. A quick glance of the mismatched, tightly packed spines told Beth not one of the journals was identical. Each volume varied in length, width, and color. Even the texture of the leathers looked unique. Some of them had the tattered paper sticking out from the top where something had been folded up and added while others had different widths of black ribbon acting as bookmarks.

She reached out to pluck one at random for closer inspection but stopped when she felt her feet get wet. Suddenly, Beth was standing in a puddle.

FIVE

BETH DIDN'T THINK ABOUT NEEDING certain things like cleaning supplies or a garbage can. Fortunately for her she was in the unique situation of moving into a place that included such luxurious amenities. She rung the mop out in the bucket what felt like a thousand times, but the floor was finally dry.

When she'd washed her dishes earlier and drained the sink, she walked away without realizing water was coming out through the bottom of the cabinet. She didn't notice until the puddle ran down the hall into the study where she stepped in it. Beth investigated to find nothing under the sink was broken, but the pipe connected to the bottom of the drain had come loose.

It was an easy, quick fix, but she would still have to make sure to double check it from time to time so the connection stayed tight. Cleaning up all the water was neither easy nor quick, and Beth cursed herself for using a full sink of water to wash two dishes. On the upside none of the floor was carpeted, which would have made for an even lengthier cleanup requiring double the effort.

The back door was in the kitchen, and Beth propped it open to dump the water from the bucket out in the grass. She turned the empty bucket upside down and set it outside to the right of the door. She did the same with the mop and propped it handle down against the house next to the bucket.

It was dark now, but the single yellow bulb in the porch light provided more than enough light to see all the way across the yard where it struggled to reach the base of the tree line. Standing just beyond the light the trees looked like angry, sharp crags shooting up from the earth to splinter the sky. As ominous as the imagery appeared, Beth found it darkly appealing, but there was something bothering her.

She couldn't put her finger on what it was right away, but once she did it was glaringly obvious. Silence. It was silent, not quiet, not peaceful, but completely silent. Not even the faintest rustling of leaves came from the trees, but stranger than that was the absence of life. There were no softly chirping crickets or buzzing cicadas or any of the sounds you would expect to hear in such close proximity to a wooded area. The summer was waning but it was still warm enough for insects to be active yet there was no sign of their presence.

Beth looked across the yard into the shadowy trees as if the reason for the silence would be somehow visibly obvious to her. She squinted into the darkness and concentrated, trying to will sound from the forest, but the silence dominated her will. She took a step off the stoop onto the grass when thunder crashed violently, like a semi-truck collision through the silence, and continued to roll with a growl as it chewed away what was left. Beth flinched and leapt back onto the stoop when the lightning flash etched its jagged, brief story across the sky.

More thunder followed, and Beth exhaled, realizing she hadn't done so for several seconds. She didn't even realize a storm was rolling in.

AMONG THE ITEMS BETH HADN'T thought to bring was a flashlight. The storm had come about suddenly and was intense from the start. Powerful gusts of wind blew down the side of the mountain and whipped fat, sloppy raindrops against the house like suicide pilots selflessly hurling themselves at their collective target.

The power had gone off almost immediately after the storm began while Beth was still standing on the stoop at the backdoor, and she stepped back in to find the house as dark as outside. She flipped the switch on the kitchen wall several times without the desired result before accepting her dark reality.

Beth dug through drawers in the kitchen as best she could without being able to see but could not find a flashlight. There were many candles scattered throughout the house, which would have made for an apt substitute if she had some way to light them. She didn't smoke so a lighter was not something she carried regularly, and she wasn't the type to grab matches at a restaurant to throw in her purse for . . . well, for a rainy day.

With as many candles as there were around the house Beth knew there had to be some way to light them, but with no way to see, looking for them seemed pointless. She hoped it wasn't a blown fuse or a tripped breaker because fixing either of those would require a visit to the basement, or at least Beth figured it would.

The fuse box in her mother's home was located in the basement, so she assumed the same would be true for this house as well. Either way, no power meant she wouldn't be able to see in the basement, and if the fuse box happened to be located elsewhere in the house, she wouldn't be able to find it without light.

She stood in the middle of the kitchen trying to think when she realized how tired she was. She'd spent the last several hours moving, and she of course didn't sleep much the night before due to the excitement of her impending independence. Fatigue slowly coiled around Beth, and she didn't attempt to struggle against its tight, suffocating grasp.

Another clap of thunder rattled her train of thought right off the tracks, and Beth decided she'd have to wait until morning to do anything about the power. Maybe in the light of day she'd be able to find matches and take a candle down to the basement to check the fuses. If all else failed she could drive a couple miles down the road and buy a flashlight at the combination grocery/hardware store she passed on her way in.

Since reading was off the table she relented to her exhaustion and began to move slowly through the darkness to the bedroom but stopped when she reached the door. She didn't know why, and she thought for sure it had something to do with her eyes adjusting, but it looked a shade or two darker in the bedroom. The entire house was dark, yes, but beyond the bedroom door it was black as pitch.

Beth lingered for a moment, daring her feet to push past the threshold, but instead they backed up and redirected her to the living room. She blindly grabbed at the air in front of her until her fingers found the side of the couch and she was able to guide herself to it. Beth pulled down the afghan she remembered seeing folded on the back of the couch, wrapped it around her shoulders, and lay down.

She thought it would be hard to fall asleep in an unfamiliar place, but a few seconds later she had already started to drift. The wind had slowed down, the raindrops much less intense, the fury of their sporadic cacophony shifting into a calming rhythm. The thunder's growl softened as it rode the storm off the mountain into town, and a second later Beth was fast asleep.

Beth dreamed she was standing in front of a fire burning in the center of a clearing in the woods, or at least she assumed so since she was surrounded by trees on all sides. They were the kind of trees you would expect from a dream in that they were clearly trees, but not like any Beth would ever see in her waking life.

The bark was black, like they'd been recently burned, but the texture said otherwise. Instead of brittle, charred chunks, the trees were smooth with somewhat of a shine reflecting the light of the fire. The branches were gnarled and bare and reached out with bone-thin, finger-like, leafless limbs beckoning her deeper into the woods.

It was dark. Beth was naked and staring across the fire at what looked like herself. She held her hands out in front of her but didn't recognize what she saw. She looked down and saw the flat, semi-toned stomach she'd worked so hard to maintain had been replaced by a wrinkly paunch with a line of wispy, white pubic hair working its way up to her naval. The sides of her stomach pulled outward and down, becoming wide hips striped with pinkish-red stretch marks like she'd been clawed at the waist by a large-pawed jungle cat.

Her breasts were big, heavy, pendulous flesh bags that sagged low enough for the large dark-colored nipples to scrape the top of her bloated stomach. Beth's hands were plump, wrinkled appendages with black, sharp fingernails jutting from the tips. She liked to keep her fingernails in good condition, but they'd never been this long and the color looked too natural to be polish. The upper portion of her arms was muscle-free, jelly-like, and swung slightly when she lifted them.

Beth looked up from a body she didn't recognize and across the fire to one she was quite familiar with. The look on her face, the 'her' who Beth was currently staring at, was dark and unfamiliar. She was smiling but not quite. It was more like a smirk, the kind of expression that typically communicates devious intent.

She tried to speak to her nude doppelganger, but her mouth would not open. She brought a hand to her lips to find them sewn shut by what felt like metallic sutures. The Beth across the fire brought a single finger up to her lips in a shushing motion but made no accompanying sound.

She watched her naked dream self turn away from the fire and walk toward the trees where she reached out, put her hand on something, and pulled. It was a door. She had opened a door from out of thin air, and inside was more darkness.

She turned back toward the fire and used the finger she'd shushed with to beckon Beth to follow. From out of nowhere a loud pounding sounded through the woods, and the ground shook before it opened up to swallow her. As she fell, the dream evaporated around her, and she opened her eyes to the sound of someone knocking on the front door.

SEVEN

SLEEP HAD DRIED IN BETH'S eyes, making them hard to open. The lids of her right eye pulled apart partially, but the left stayed stuck tight. She rubbed the heels of her palms into them to sufficiently break the sticky seal and unknot her eyelashes.

Awake and able to see without obstruction, Beth was confused and disoriented, partially from being in a new place, but more so because of the dream she'd had. It seemed so real she swore she could still feel heat from the fire on her skin, and she suddenly grabbed at her chest and midsection, relieved to find she still maintained her own proportions.

The pounding on the door came again, startling Beth into nearly jumping off the couch to duck and cover. She remembered now the knocking was what woke her up in the first place. She sighed, relieved, but the feeling was short-lived and replaced by anxious, angry curiosity when the knock came again, harder this time, cementing her back in reality indefinitely.

Beth threw the afghan off and narrowed her eyes at the door, exhaling through a pout. She knew she should feel pensive about opening it, but the logic part of her brain hadn't fully come online as she stomped over to the door.

She turned the deadbolt, grabbed the handle, and yanked with no plan other than to express her disdain for whoever was knocking to their face, which would more than likely include explicit and colorful language. The aggravation evaporated when she found herself face to face with her mother.

Without missing a beat Beth stepped forward and wrapped her mother in an uncharacteristic and unexpected embrace. It wasn't that she and her mom weren't affectionate toward each other, but it had never been approached with such enthusiasm. Beth's aggressive reception of her mother wasn't because she already missed her; she'd only been gone one day, after all. It was a comfort Beth didn't know she needed until she saw her mother, and it all of a sudden became glaringly obvious.

"Jesus, Beth! Just tackle me why don't you!"

"Sorry," Beth said, pulling her head from her mother's shoulder and stepping back into the house. "It's . . . uh, seeing you is a nice surprise, that's all."

"Well," her mother said, following Beth into the house, "after you left I got to thinking about what kind of mother would send their daughter off into the woods without any means of communication?"

"What are you talking about?" Beth walked through the living room to the kitchen, looking over her shoulder. "Oh, do you want some coffee?"

As soon as she said it Beth realized that unless Aunt Agnes left some coffee around there would be none to have, and if the electricity were still out it wouldn't matter anyway. She turned around to find her mother right behind with her hand in her purse from which she pulled out Beth's cellphone.

"I'm talking about this," she said, holding up the phone. "After you left I realized I didn't know if this place had a landline, and even if it did I wouldn't know the number. I decided to let you hold onto this, but only until you're able to start paying for one on your own. Understand?"

She tried to use her best motherly tone to convey to Beth she was serious about paying for her own phone, but something in her mother's eyes softened her remark. At first she thought it was her way of showing she already missed Beth or was having some difficulty with the idea of her not living at home anymore, but as she took the phone from her mother's hand she realized it wasn't that at all.

It was fear.

She wasn't expressing anything as extreme as abject terror, but there was a subtle flash in her eyes Beth recognized. She'd seen the same look all those years ago at the picnic when her mother yanked Beth away from Aunt Agnes. She'd masked it with anger then, and this time with concern, but Beth could see through both attempts. She took the phone from the outstretched hand of her mother and decided she wouldn't ruin the visit by bringing it up now.

"Thank you," Beth said, looking from her mom to the phone and back.

She held her thumb on the power button, but the screen refused to come to life. Beth looked up and saw the kitchen light was on. She hadn't realized it earlier because the light it gave off disappeared in the brightness of the sun.

"Oh, thank Christ," Beth said to the ceiling.

"What? What is it?" Beth's mother was looking up, searching for what had grabbed her daughter's attention.

"The lights," Beth said, dialing back her excitement. "The storm last night knocked out the power, and I was worried it might have been a fuse. I didn't have a flashlight, and I couldn't find any matches or a lighter so I just went to sleep. I was hoping to avoid having to go into the basement to check the fuse box."

The concern lifted from her mother's face, and she turned to look around the small kitchen area, taking in the quaint surroundings of her late sister's home. Her back was to Beth when she paused briefly and tried unsuccessfully to stifle a shudder. Beth saw the muscles in her back tense and spasm through the fabric of her blouse as she leveled her gaze at the door to the basement.

"You haven't been," Beth's mother paused, her back still to Beth, "down there, have you?"

Her mother's body language and tone changed in that moment, and although Beth couldn't see her face, she imagined a fearful expression upon it and not the sly smile she was actually wearing.

"No, not yet," Beth replied slowly, hoping her mother had an explanation for the question. "Like I said, I was hoping to not have to go down there at all, and since the power is back on it looks like I won't have to, at least for the time being. To be honest, I haven't even tried to open the door."

Before Beth could comprehend what her mother was doing, let alone react, it had already happened. She had bounded across the kitchen to the basement door and grabbed the knob.

"Mom—" Beth began but that was all her brain was able to push through her mouth.

The door didn't budge, but Beth's mother rattled and pulled the knob a few more times to no avail.

"What are you doing?" Beth finally managed, slapping a hand down on her mother's shoulder.

She didn't realize she'd crossed the kitchen until she'd touched her mother and felt the spasms rushing up and down her back. It was brief, but in that moment Beth realized she didn't know how to be there for her mother if she was truly frightened of something.

24

Her mom had always been the strong, no nonsense person that comforted Beth and helped her realize she had nothing to be afraid of.

She swung around to face Beth, wearing a familiar smile that betrayed everything Beth was feeling about the interaction.

"Well, it looks like the door is locked anyway," her mother said, sliding from her daughter's grip over to the sink. "It's just as well. Probably nothing but cobwebs and critters anyway."

Beth looked at the doorknob and then over to her mother, picturing the ugly, sharp-toothed, insatiable creatures that ate everything in their path, knowing full well her mother wasn't referring to the movie *Critters*, but the visual made her smile.

"Uh . . . yeah," Beth said. "Just as well."

Beth's mother stayed for almost four hours. It was much longer than Beth expected, but she didn't mind since having her mother there helped the house not feel so foreign. She brought a warm and cleansing energy with her that dispelled the discomfort Beth felt in the unfamiliar space.

The house hadn't been shut up for long after Aunt Agnes died, but Beth hadn't noticed the staleness in the air until her mother arrived to counteract it in a way only moms can do. She'd also gone around the entire house and opened all the windows, which might have had something to do with it as well.

Her mother helped her unpack the few things she hadn't done the night before, which wasn't much and didn't take long. Beth was glad the house came with so much stuff because otherwise it would be a sad, empty sight. There wouldn't have been a couch to sleep on or any other furniture, for that matter. Aunt Agnes's old furniture worked for now, but she was already making mental notes of what she wanted to replace and roughly how much she'd need to save.

After the two spent much longer than necessary arranging Beth's modest amount of belongings she figured her mother would be ready to leave, but she didn't. Normally her mother was not an incredibly warm person or one to stay anywhere longer than she needed to, so her behavior was confusing. In fact, Beth expected she'd leave long before lunchtime, yet here they were sitting on the front porch eating sandwiches her mother insisted upon making.

While this was out of character, Beth wasn't put off by it and quietly decided she'd rather enjoy than question. Perhaps her mom's steely, clinical coldness was softened by a sudden bout of empty nest syndrome. Beth hadn't had time to give it much thought, but now, as she sat next to her mother eating sandwiches with only peanut butter because there was no jelly, she too felt a pang of homesickness.

"Why weren't you and Aunt Agnes close? Did something happen?"

The thought leapt from Beth's mind and out of her mouth with no delay between the two. It was something she'd thought about since the house was signed over to her, but fearing a bad reaction from her mother, she chose not to ask about it.

She hadn't planned on asking her now either, but it almost seemed she had no control over the matter. Her desire to know overruled the fear of a possible confrontation and forced the question out. Beth squirmed in her chair, anticipating an unpleasant reaction, but she felt like she needed to know. She was living in the woman's house now, after all, which she felt warranted at least a cursory explanation of the distance between the two.

The question hung for a moment between the two women like a volleyed balloon. Beth's mother prolonged the tense moment by taking extra time to chew the bite of sandwich in her mouth.

"I didn't have anything against her," she said flatly after swallowing. "She was my sister, after all."

Surprised by her mother's tame response, Beth felt a little more confident continuing to prod for information.

"You could've fooled me."

Beth tensed again, expecting her flippancy to be met with sharp scolding, but again she'd assumed incorrectly. With nothing to chew, her mother released a deep sigh to prolong the moment before her answer.

Beth watched her mother's eyes narrow and the skin on her face pull into a tight, ambiguous expression.

"Your aunt," she began, "well, she . . . she had a tendency to want things her way, and she wanted me to do things her way as well. It got to the point where she needed to control every aspect of our time together, which was the majority of it since we lived together at the time. I finally moved out and enjoyed being away from her so much I just kept it that way."

Beth wasn't completely satisfied with the vague answer but knew better than to push any further. She'd learned that lesson through countless similar interactions between the two of them throughout the years.

It was the most information her mother had ever divulged concerning her relationship with Aunt Agnes, so Beth wisely chose to let the issue die. She figured her best bet was to let some time pass, and maybe on the next visit her mother made, or even the one after that, she would broach the subject again.

Her mother sat up straight on the edge of her chair and stared off into the yard past the trees and down the driveway. Beth tried to follow her mother's sightline to see what had so intently captured her focus but saw nothing out of the ordinary. When Beth turned back to her mother the woman was standing in front of her chair, empty plate dangling limply from her right hand.

Beth absently shoved the last bite of sandwich in her mouth and spoke through a dry lump of peanut butter and bread. "Are you leaving?" She took a quick sip from the glass of water balanced on the arm of her chair to help swallow the larger than average bite.

"Yeah, I think it's about that time," she said, still gazing off down the long gravel driveway.

Beth continued to chew vigorously while wiping her hands on the back of her jeans. Her jaw ached from trying to rush the mastication process so she could verbalize her thanks, but the process was laboriously slow. Her mother waited patiently, still looking down the driveway and back while scanning the yard and trees again.

"You said a storm knocked out the power last night?" She continued to survey the lawn as she spoke.

"Ye–yeah," Beth coughed as the last chunk of peanut butter slid down her throat. "Yeah, it was a bad one, too. The rain was coming down in sheets! I've heard people use that expression in the past, but now it totally makes sense. I'm surprised you didn't get any rain down in town?"

Beth's mother didn't say anything right away, but a few seconds later she clicked her tongue, shrugged her shoulders, and turned to go back inside the house to retrieve her purse.

"What?" Beth asked, looking out into the yard, trying to see what it was her mother was seeing. "What did you mean by that?"

"The grass isn't wet," she said.

EIGHT

BETH WALKED BAREFOOT THROUGH THE backyard, heading for the tree line. The grass was cooler than it was out front since the sun had sunk low enough for the trees to cast dark and distorted shadows across the yard all the way to the back of the house. While a few degrees cooler, it was as dry as the grass in the front yard.

For a while after her mother left Beth stood barefoot in the lawn only a few feet from the porch. She paced up and down, working her way from one side to the other, convinced she was steps away from finding a low-lying spot where water from the storm had collected, but each step was as dry and level as the last.

The cool grass was ankle high, and Beth smashed small portions of it flat with each stomp of her bare feet. When she reached the trees she stopped, and without hesitating thrust her hand up, grabbing ahold of the closest branch. She wrapped her fingers around it and shook the branch as violently as the give of the limb would allow. She expected to be showered by the drops of water still clinging to the leaves, but all that fell was two dry, dead leaves.

She walked the tree line, furiously grabbing and shaking low hanging limbs, getting the same results. She finally gave up and stopped to catch her breath, not yet realizing she'd started crying. She wasn't bawling, but tears of frustration were staining lines down her cheek where they cut through the dust and pollen that settled there from all the branch shaking.

Beth knew it had stormed last night, she absolutely knew it, yet there was no evidence of the fact. Was it possible she *didn't* know? The only explanation she could imagine was a scenario in which she'd fallen asleep soon after moving her things in and the storm had been a dream, but that would mean she'd also dreamt all of her other experiences leading up to the storm.

The memories were so clear in her mind, it had to have really happened.

With her breathing and tears now under control the still, cold silence clamped down so hard it was jarring. Beth hadn't been thinking about it upon first stomping through the yard, but now, against the contrast of the ruckus she'd created, it was impossible not to notice. The quiet was far from comforting and carried weight that pushed down on Beth, making it hard to walk.

A lump of fear leapt into Beth's throat, and her legs felt heavier than normal, as if the limbs didn't belong to her anymore. The entire lower half of her body remained visibly unchanged but felt like it had been replaced by bulky and cumbersome exaggerations of what legs were supposed to be.

A piercing, sharp whistle from somewhere deep in the woods ruptured the silence. The whistling stopped suddenly but started back after only half a second's respite, this time louder, shriller. Beth fought the urge to turn her head and look back. She kept her eyes straight, pointed directly at the backdoor where, if she were given back control of her legs, she would sprint straight through and lock behind her.

The whistle stopped again for the same short amount of time, and when it came again louder, clearly closer, a single tear rolled from her left eye down to her chin where it hung, refusing to let go, lingering in its death throes. What came next wasn't a whistle; this time it was a scream. A long, high-pitched, screeching moan of a scream wracked with the pain of desperation, and it sounded close.

A shiver started from below Beth's stomach and subtly vibrated its way to the top of her head. The shudder broke the teardrop's hold on her chin, and as it fell Beth realized she suddenly had control over her legs again. No longer were they held in place by invisible, foreign influence, and upon feeling them flood with sensation, Beth ran. She didn't hear the scream again before making it to the backdoor, but her head was filled with the deafening pounding of her heart and gasping breaths.

Her hand landed on the doorknob a foot before her body did and she twisted, hoping she'd left the door unlocked. Mercifully, the knob turned and the door opened in time for Beth to fall inside, roll over on her back, and kick it shut behind her. She hurried to her knees and lunged forward to engage the deadbolt.

Beth sunk to the floor with her back against the door and shook with sobs, questioning for the first time if she really was ready to live on her own.

NINE

IT WAS DARK OUTSIDE WHEN Beth wrung the sponge in the sink one final time before leaning it against the faucet to dry. Over the last few hours she had detail cleaned the kitchen from top to bottom. It was a tedious chore that would've needed to be done at some point, but Beth decided to give it immediate attention. The main purpose was to distract her from thinking about what she'd experienced in the backyard earlier.

Unfortunately, the chore had quite the opposite effect as her mind worked to dissect what happened while her body cleaned on autopilot. The benefit to this undesired result forced Beth to scrutinize and therefore use a malleable form of logic to justify the occurrence. She decided she *had* experienced the storm the night before, basing her certainty on her memories of the journals in the study, which she double-checked were indeed there.

The explanation was quite simple once she really thought about it. The grass was no longer wet because it had time to dry, more than enough time, in fact. Beth and her mother had talked and arranged her things inside for hours before they'd gone out to the porch. Even there they talked for at least forty-five minutes before her mother made the comment.

The sun had been out all day, and the house sat on an incline so the water must have run right down into the street. The branches were all dry because what water hadn't evaporated dropped to the ground and drained away. It was that simple, that easy of an explanation. Frankly, Beth felt foolish for having such an emotional reaction and was glad her mother hadn't seen her break down.

The scream, though, the scream was harder to come up with an explanation for. She finally decided it was only the wind. There were tree limbs in the forest randomly tangled together in such a way to create the high-pitched sound as air passed through. It was only wishful thinking because Beth knew it wasn't the wind. The backyard had been as still and stiflingly silent as it was the night before.

She was two and a half hours into her cleaning spree, standing on a step stool vigorously scrubbing shelves in one of the cabinets, when she realized what it was. There was no scream. What Beth heard, or rather thought she heard, was a byproduct of the stress-induced panic she'd fallen into. It was an auditory hallucination brought on by the duress of freaking out.

It was such a simple explanation Beth almost believed it, and after a half hour or so of convincing herself, any lingering doubt was removed. By the time she'd finished with the shelves and was putting the coffee mugs back where they belonged she was absolutely sure she'd imagined the scream.

BETH STOOD IN THE DOORWAY of the room-turned-study for nearly ten full minutes before stepping inside. She was taking time to thoroughly scan everything about the room from the only vantage point that allowed her to see it all at once. She wasn't sure what she was looking for, or why, but she felt the need to at least familiarize herself with every inch of the room from top to bottom.

The brief glance she'd given the room a few hours earlier after the incident in the backyard was to reaffirm she had indeed been in the room the night before and therefore could not have dreamt up the storm and power outage. Now standing in the door to the study she couldn't beat back the odd, uncomfortable feeling that reached out of the darkness and grabbed her.

She felt a nagging pull at the bottom of her stomach that created a mild cramping sensation up her midsection where it hit her diaphragm. The feeling then dropped back down, knotting itself to her small intestine, creating a unique tension she felt through her whole body. It was not a pleasant feeling.

Nothing looked out of the ordinary about the room, and nothing seemed different from what she could remember seeing the day before. It was a modest setup for an aging spinster to keep the books she'd collected in her life, as well as a place Aunt Agnes herself could sit in a quiet, comfortable space to write her own thoughts down. She may have been an aspiring writer who spent the majority of her days in the room filling her various leather-bound journals with fantastical stories or perhaps the story of her own life.

Beth still hadn't had a chance to look through any of the journals, but she intended to. She felt compelled to dive into the many volumes her aunt left behind and hoped what she found inside could shed more light on the relationship she and Beth's mother had.

She stepped in the room, toward the desk, and the tension in her body tightened like a spring around her spine the closer she got. Before she knew it, Beth had snatched one of the journals randomly and was already back out in the hall, running her hands across the aged leather over and over as if it was a texture so foreign her hands could not compute its existence.

Beth closed the door to the study, deciding she would keep it that way unless she was using the room for something. Maybe she'd leave it open during the daytime, but for now she planned to keep it closed at night.

Despite the excitement of the day Beth had effectively worked off all her nervous energy thanks to the impromptu deep clean. Her plan was to get ready for bed and peruse the journal for a little while until her eyes got too heavy to read. She hoped to settle herself enough to fall asleep quickly, and reading in bed always helped the process along.

Beth took the book into the bedroom across the hall where she would sleep for the first time and where she would continue to sleep for the remainder of her time in the house. She'd gone into the bedroom earlier, before retrieving her reading material, and turned down the bed, surprised by how clean the sheets were. They even smelled freshly laundered.

Beth wasn't one for nightgowns or pajamas, preferring to sleep naked, and after placing the journal on the nightstand she peeled off her clothes and kicked them over against the wall. She'd worked up a sweat with all the cleaning but was too tired to worry about it now and would shower in the morning.

The sheets were cool and smooth against her skin, much smoother than the sheets she slept on back home. Beth pulled them up to her neck, opting to fold the comforter down to the foot of the bed since she wasn't cold and absolutely hated being hot while sleeping. She took a moment to nestle herself in, reveling in the overall comfort of what was now *her* bed before reaching over for the journal.

She turned it over in her hands again a few times, enjoying the tactile sensation of the dry, cracked leather as she rested it on her stomach. Beth had a twinge of anxiety before opening the book, as if she were about to read her own medical test results instead of the mystery journaling of an old, dead woman.

She shook the feeling away and opened the book to a random page in the middle. Beth frowned and furrowed her brow before turning the page, then turning it again, and finally fanning the pages as she flipped through them all.

The pages were filled with hand-drawn symbols and sigils, and any text she found was neither in English nor any other tongue Beth was familiar with. There were sketches of fire and half-finished body parts running up and down the margins of some pages. Beth wondered what significance they held, if any, or if they were simply the product of a lazy daydream. The rest of the pages were filled from top to bottom with no room for additional adornment.

She sighed and let the journal fall off her stomach onto the bed next to her. She entertained the thought of getting up to grab one or several more of the journals, but a moment of hesitation was all it took for fatigue to finally wrestle Beth down into a deep, restful sleep.

———————

Beth's sleep started off dreamless, her subconscious shellacked in an inky, impenetrable darkness. At some point the opaque coating pealed away, and a grainy scene came into focus within the depths of her rem sleep. It started out in the absurd, surrealistic way dreams do where the setting is familiar but not really, and the people you encounter are slightly different than in your waking life.

Beth's mother was in the dream, and the two of them were in the kitchen talking like they had been that afternoon. It looked like the kitchen in the house Beth now resided in only the sizes of the cabinets and doorways were greatly exaggerated to the point of being cartoonish.

Beth turned around to pour herself more tea from a kettle that was an oversize snail shell when she heard her mother say her name.

"Yes, Mother," she said, turning back around.

The teacup vanished from her hand at the same time Beth realized her mother was also gone.

"Beth."

This time it came from behind where she'd been filling her tea. When she spun back around she still didn't see her mother, but through the window over the sink she saw trees right up against the pane like thick wooden burglar bars.

"Beth," came the call again.

Beth spun on her heel, and the ceiling disappeared. Her mother's voice continued to call her name from all sides as more and more of the kitchen was pulled away to reveal the encroaching forest. The cabinets went next, followed by the sink, refrigerator, counter, and then the rest of the walls. With the kitchen completely gone, Beth found herself in the same clearing from her dream the prior, except for one thing.

The basement door remained and was separated from Beth by the fire that suddenly flared up between them. Her dream wasn't exactly the same, but she ended up in the same place as the night before. She looked down at her hands and arms to find they hadn't gone saggy and plump with age, and she appeared to be herself this time.

"Beth."

The voice was calling to her from behind the door. There was no mistaking it. She scanned the circle of trees around her, searching for any possible threat, but beyond the initial ring was nothing but thick, syrupy darkness.

"Beth."

She took a step toward the fire and it roared as if agitated by her proximity but just as quickly shrunk back, giving her a clear view of the door. It suddenly swung open, and a scream ripped the cold silence apart, splitting it down the center to release the cacophony beneath. The scream was coming from Beth, but she wasn't cognizant of it. Suddenly the entire scene was being sucked into the open door like water being forced down a drain. First the trees went, then the grass, and then the fire.

It happened so fast Beth didn't realize she was flying headlong through the door until her head caught up with the flames.

Beth woke up when she hit the floor, having rolled off the bed from flailing in her sleep. She landed hard on her back with her head close behind, but the thick area rug the bed sat on helped to lessen the impact. Her hands shot to her head, working to beat down dream-flames that never existed.

By the time she'd come to her senses her hair was knotted and bunched around her ears. Beth sat up and carefully worked her fingers through the tangles, trying not to pull any hair out in the process. When she'd done all she could do without the aid of a brush Beth pulled herself up on the bed and perched from the side of it.

It took a few seconds to shake the dream completely and realize she was indeed awake. Beth absently rubbed the top and sides of her head to relieve the lingering sensation of phantom fire. She knew it was all a dream, but the vividness haunted her. Beth absently massaged the sides of her bare thighs while telling herself to calm down.

"Get it together," she scolded herself. "You've only been on your own for two days, and you're already trying to scare yourself into going back home."

This was the only way Beth could rationalize having two nearly identical, terrifying dreams. The unfamiliarity of her new surroundings had triggered a homesickness that manifested itself in a couple creepy, weird nightmares. It was a stretch and Beth knew it, but it was the stretch she needed to preserve her sanity.

Beth put her arms down behind her to lean back, and her right hand landed on the open journal she had abandoned the night before. She picked it up and set the book on her lap, staring down at the page it was open to. It was one of many with odd illustrations in the margins like she'd seen last night, but this one was slightly different.

Fire was a prominent element of this border, as depicted by the wispy, arching flames that weaved their way through the gnarled and blackened branches, the foliage long since burned away. Beth shook her head and smiled as she traced a finger down the edge of the page.

Well, that explains it, she told to herself. *I wish I could tell my subcon-*

scious to chill out on the nightmares until I'm a little more comfortable here, at least.

Beth determined the page the book was open to was the last one she'd looked at before falling asleep, and therefore the images had subconsciously informed her dream. That's why she was in the forest again and why she ended up going headfirst into the fire. The door was there again because, well, it was on her mind. She still hadn't gone into the basement and her hesitance and curiosity showed through in the dream as well.

All of this made sense to her despite the conclusions she was drawing based on no real knowledge or expertise in the field of dreams, but it helped set her at ease. Still, the smallest perceptible amount of doubt nagged at Beth from somewhere below her stomach.

She went to close the journal before standing up but paused to look one more time. Beth had been focused on what bordered the page, but now she took a moment to examine the illustration as a whole. A drawing of a raging bonfire in the center of the page appeared to be the cause of the burning border, but it was what was in the fire that truly caught her attention.

In the center was the dark form of a woman who'd been swallowed by the blaze and was now part of it. Her arms were outstretched with her palms open in a welcoming gesture.

Beth closed the journal and tossed it back on the bed behind her.

ELEVEN

IT TOOK A WHILE TO get the water to heat up, and just when Beth was resigned to take a cold shower a rumbling came through the pipes, bringing a rush of heat with it. When she'd first turned the knobs the faucet spat and coughed spurts of brown water that got lighter with each burst. It was completely clear by the time the water started running free of interruption, only it was cold.

The hot water heater would of course be in the basement, and Beth thought it was quite likely the issue was the pilot light. She was going to have to relight it if she ever wanted hot water, and while she was willing to stomach one or two cold showers, it would need to be done.

The more she thought about it, Beth was glad she was going to have to light it because it gave her a very necessary reason to go into the basement. She would see there was nothing to be afraid of and be done with it. Beth suddenly remembered her mother trying to open the basement door the day before and how it had been stuck

She wracked her brain for items in the house she could use to pry the door open or even break off the knob, if that's what it took. This was when the pipes shook and bellowed before belching the warmth the hot water heater had finally seen fit to grant. It was a small relief, but as she stepped under the water she knew she wasn't off the hook.

Beth realized she'd not packed her hairdryer and could not find one amongst Aunt Agnes's toiletries, so she kept her hair down to air dry. Retrieving the hairdryer was a good reason to go back to the house, but she wasn't sure if it was a good idea.

She was afraid once she was back in her comfortable space again she might convince herself the house and living on her own wasn't what it was cracked up to be. Then she'd rationalize why it was a better idea to come back home and live with her mother again for another year until she was really ready. Still, even at her young age Beth knew there was no such thing as being 'ready' for a life event. They happened and you adapted.

She knew she didn't want to move home, but she knew herself even better. It wouldn't be the first time Beth had talked herself out of doing something because she was a little scared. The nervous tendency had robbed her of many 'formative' experiences growing up that required even the slightest amount of risk. If she wanted a hairdryer she would go down the road into town and buy one. Her old one would simply remain at her—her *mother's*— house for now, and maybe she'd retrieve it sometime in the future when she had a legitimate reason to go there.

Beth stood at the sink wearing panties and a sleeveless Behemoth t-shirt she stole from her ex-boyfriend, Noah. He claimed to be into the band, which was one of Beth's favorites, and bought the shirt at a concert he took her too on one of their early dates. When he realized how much they sung about Satan Noah suddenly lost interest and would squirm every time she played one of their records.

The relationship only lasted four and a half months with Beth becoming more and more put off by the false front Noah perpetrat-ed when he was really just a poseur mama's boy. She finally told him to pop his mom's tit out of his mouth, stop pretending to be some-thing he wasn't, and grow up. She placed a well timed 'fuck off' in there somewhere along the way.

When she went to get the few things she'd left at his place she stole the shirt as well as a stack of records he'd bought to impress her during the time they'd been dating. Several of them were still sealed in cellophane including Cattle Decapitation's *Humanure,* and Slayer's *Christ Illusion.*

They were as pristine as the day he'd bought them. One of the many times they went to the record store together. Beth remem-bered being excited with his selections, all the while not realizing he had no idea who these bands were. He'd pretended to browse while Beth was looking at records, silently cataloging her reactions to cer-tain albums. When Noah met her at the register with his final selec-tions her heart would melt at seeing how connected they were. Even now she found it hard to believe she'd been fooled.

Beth broke it off with Noah just over a year ago and hadn't dat-ed anyone since. She couldn't get over how easy it was for someone to completely fake who they were to get something, but even more so, she couldn't believe how easily she fell for it. Beth's mother comforted her the best way she knew how by telling her this hap-pens to everyone, and it was a part of life, and how she would get over it in no time, and blah, blah, blah.

Beth didn't 'get over it' with the ease her mother suggested. There was something so deeply sinister in this kind of deception and it left an indelible mark on her that no amount of motherly ad-vice could wash away. She knew it wasn't Noah's intent for his act to leave such a lasting impression, but sometimes accidents cause permanent damage.

She sipped coffee and looked out the window across the yard. It didn't seem as big in the full, unobstructed light of day, and the tree line didn't seem so distant when not partially shrouded by shadows. Taking in the pleasant scene only barely distracted Beth from what she was trying to avoid thinking about.

The electricity had come back on, and the hot water eventually worked, so she no longer had a necessarily immediate reason to venture down to the basement. She was also doing her best to shake off the odd coincidences between her dream and the drawing in her aunt's journal.

Lost in thought, Beth turned from the window and faced the kitchen, taking a moment of pride in the thorough cleaning she'd done the day before. Something she saw made her soft smile wilt, and the coffee mug slipped from her fingers, shattering at her feet. Tepid, brown liquid splashed up on her exposed legs along with small ceramic shards that left dozens of tiny, red slits.

The basement door was open.

———

Beth's first instinct had been to go for the broom and dustpan she'd leaned in the corner across the kitchen the night before. She stepped on broken pieces of the shattered mug in the process and hopped the rest of the way to the wall. She stopped there and looked across the room toward the basement door, breaking from her pre-conditioned response to clean up.

She hadn't imagined it. The door was indeed open and a half-inch strip of darkness now separated it from the frame. She ignored the burning cut on the bottom of her foot, able to focus only on the basement door. Her rational mind told her there had to be a simple explanation as to how it opened on its own, but she wasn't sure how much she trusted that part of herself anymore.

Still, the house was old so there was the possibility it had something to do with humidity or with the kitchen being back in use after an extended hiatus, what with the fluctuating temperature. These were uneducated guesses though, since Beth didn't have any real knowledge of such things.

She was struck with a realization that tugged her bowels down into her groin. What if the door was open because someone came through from the other side? Beth had walked around the day before, but she didn't take time to notice if there was a door outside of the house that granted access to the basement. The thought someone could be in the house with her sank a sharp, cold pang of paralyzing fear that split her down the middle.

"H-hello?"

Her voice was barely a quaver, but the house was small enough for her to have been heard throughout. She listened intently for breathing or shuffling or anything that would betray the location of her would-be intruder, but there was nothing. She wasn't even sure what she would do if someone answered or, worse, lunged out from the closet or behind a door.

Her phone was sitting on the sink in the bathroom where she'd left it after her shower. She'd intended to pour her coffee and return to finish getting ready, but that was before she'd seen the door. Beth would have to run across the kitchen, past the basement door, down the hall, and through the bedroom to get it, leaving her vulnerable to attack by surprise or not.

She looked back toward the sink where she'd been standing and then to the door to the backyard next to it. But then what? She still wouldn't have her phone, and it wasn't like there was a neighbor she could run to for help. Aunt Agnes's house was isolated where it stood at the base of the mountain, and while other houses dotted the surrounding area, Beth would have to run through patches of forest for miles before she came to another home, and that was only if she was heading in the right direction.

She could run around the house, make her way down the driveway, and hope to flag down one of the few and far between motorists who happened by, but it could literally be hours before she'd see one. The keys to her own vehicle were on an end table by the door in the living room, which was farther than her phone. She'd be left vulnerable for a longer period of time but only by a few seconds, and getting the keys would be more valuable than the phone.

If she could get them and make it to the Cherokee unscathed she'd be able to lock herself in, gun it the hell out of there, and get help herself rather than calling for it. Either way she went, if there was someone hiding in the house that meant Beth harm, they were already a step up on her.

She felt something wet and warm beneath her feet and looked down to see a crimson puddle slowly pushing its way out from under them. She picked her left foot up and reached down to pull a thick sliver of the broken mug out from where it had punctured and then lodged itself in the soft center. She'd been too numb with fear to realize the steps she'd taken sunk the shard deeper, resulting in the free-bleeding gash.

Beth stared at the bloody glass between her fingers and watched it quiver as she began to shake trying to keep from having an all-out bawling meltdown. She kept the sobs in check, swallowing hard to push the lump back down her throat, but she wasn't able to stop the tears.

Suddenly, a bang like a gunshot shook the room and ruptured the tense silence as a blackbird smacked against the kitchen window. Beth screamed, flinched, and inadvertently stepped forward on her injured foot. She slid first and then stumbled before falling into the basement door with her shoulder slamming it shut once again.

After she'd tripped into the basement door Beth's fight or flight instinct took over, the flight side primarily. If someone were in the house, this would be the perfect opportunity to attack while she struggled to regain balance on an injured foot. There was no more time for her to analyze her options and weigh pros and cons.

Beth stood shakily and pushed away from the door, propelling herself into the hall, limping as fast as she could. The house was small, but in that moment the front door seemed miles away. Beth could see the table next to the door, and upon it sat the keys where she'd left them. She held the wall with her left arm for support as she limped, pulling it back only for a moment when she passed the study.

Tears streamed down her cheeks with renewed vigor as she told herself she didn't see it. She needed to get to the keys and the door, and that was all she had the capacity to process at this time. It was an illusion. The angles of shadows caused by the direction of the light created the dark figure Beth saw from the corner of her eye crouched up against the bookshelf when she passed by.

She sped up, putting her full weight on her injured foot now as the recent fresh dump of adrenaline had overridden any physical pain. She reached for the keys but was unable to slow her panic-induced momentum, and it carried her into the table head first with her arms out. She managed to turn herself so her shoulder took the brunt of the collision with the legs of the table, which snapped as she hit them, helping to absorb some of the impact.

The fall barely registered with Beth, and she pushed herself to her feet in an instant, like she'd rehearsed the move for weeks. The keys lay within the wreckage of busted table legs, and Beth bent down to pluck them from the mess before pulling the front door open and sprinting for the Jeep, injured foot be damned.

She'd been stabbing the button on the key fob with her thumb to unlock the doors since she picked it up, and now that she sat behind the wheel knowing full well the doors were locked she couldn't help hitting the button on her console again and again.

Beth put the key in the ignition, but didn't start the engine. She sat behind the steering wheel shaking with sobs. She expected someone or something to burst from the open front door at any second, but the seconds passed and nothing happened. The more seconds that passed the less Beth shook. An hour went by before she was able to fully stay her spasms and convince herself no one was coming after her because no one had been in the house to begin with.

She thought a lot while locked in the Jeep, mostly about what happened prior to her taking refuge. It was quiet in the car, but not the same quiet she'd noticed in the backyard. That quiet was eerie and unnatural while in the Jeep it was comforting and warm. Beth felt like she could think clearly for the first time in the last two days and set to dissecting what happened in the kitchen.

It all started with the basement door being open. She'd dropped the mug, cut her foot, and locked herself in the Jeep because of that goddamn door. With the adrenaline wearing off, Beth could feel her shoulder throb and stiffen.

She slowly rolled it back and forth within the socket, hoping she hadn't done any real damage, and while it was sore, the mobility meant it wasn't broken. There would be a large, ugly bruise left behind, without a doubt, but she could deal with bruises.

The cut on her foot was a different story as a sharp, jabbing pain set in to the injured area. Beth never had stitches before so she wasn't sure if she needed them, but she'd never had a cut this bad either. It wasn't bleeding as freely anymore but only because dirt and grass had stuck to the cut on her way through the yard.

The bottom of her foot stung from grit that had worked its way up inside, increasing the chance of infection. Reluctantly, Beth decided she needed to go back inside and take care of her foot. No one had come rushing out of the house with a machete or hatchet, and if they were still hiding inside trying to play the long game, Beth thought they deserved to get another chance at her for their patience alone.

She stepped outside, shut the door, and limped around the car. She stopped at the steps to the porch as the memory of what she'd seen lurking in the shadows of the bookcase suddenly hit her.

The instance was so brief Beth beat back the thought by reminding herself it was just the shadows and nothing more. Still, being attacked by a backwoods, *Hills Have Eyes* kind of person would be favorable to what she saw—or thought she saw—in the study.

When she walked back into the house it certainly looked like an attack had occurred, but Beth had done all the damage herself. The table lay in pieces strewn from the door to the couch like it had been smashed against someone's back in a bar fight. It was clearly beyond repair.

There were red splotches of blood marking her path from the kitchen, through the hall, and to the door, each step a Rorschach test in its own right.

She approached the kitchen slowly, her eyes darting directly to the basement door, which was still closed. She turned to the rest of the kitchen and her heart sank. Pieces of broken coffee cup and the cold liquid remnants it held were spread across the floor in front of the sink where she'd dropped it. There were streaks of blood in various stages of drying that marked her progression across the kitchen.

It was like she'd created a much gorier version of marking a trail with breadcrumbs that dared pursuers to follow. The sliver she'd pulled from the bottom of her foot was still where she dropped it. The bloodstain had turned the ceramic a rosy pink color.

Her stomach lurched, and Beth turned to limp to the bathroom holding a hand over her mouth. She made it through the bedroom and stepped into the bathroom in time to heave her guts out onto the closed toilet seat lid.

TWELVE

BETH STEPPED OUT INTO THE backyard from the kitchen holding a folded paper grocery sack she'd found under the sink. She was re-showered and fully dressed now, and her left foot was wrapped tightly with supplies found in a first-aid kit beneath the bathroom sink. She let the door close behind her and looked out across the backyard, thinking how much smaller it seemed compared to when she'd first laid eyes on it. Beth supposed it was a trick of her over-stimulated, over-excited brain trying to process the idea of her actual independence.

Five feet to her right lay the dead bird. The thing was black but didn't look like a crow, which was the only type of black bird she knew. Even now as she tried to picture one she realized her main source material were a pair of animated crows in the old *Looney Tunes* episodes she watched reruns of as a child. Outside of that she really had no knowledge of the avian species.

The bird's neck was bent at a sharp, unnatural angle down against its side. The wing beneath its head remained tucked against its body while the other was splayed out across the ground, the tiny hollow bones snapped in several places. Loose black feathers stuck to the grass around the broken animal as well as directly below the point of impact.

There were no cracks in the window from the incident; there was barely even a mark. The only evidence it happened was a smudge the size of a pencil eraser left by the bird's eye when it smacked the glass.

Beth had already cleaned the messes she'd made in the bathroom, living room, and kitchen. She'd saved this particular bit for last, and even now wished she could delay the act further. It wasn't handling the dead bird that bothered Beth, but the fear associated with it still echoed through her body and mind. She was afraid touching it would reignite the feeling in a way she wouldn't be able to come back from.

She pulled the cellphone from her back pocket, opened her contacts, and scrolled to the one she'd almost called a dozen times in the last hour, her mother. She didn't want her mom to think she couldn't handle being on her own, but at the same time she desperately craved the comfort only a mother could provide.

She'd almost placed the call to her mother right after she'd gotten sick. Beth was sitting in vomit crying when she pulled the phone down from the sink and made a mess of the screen trying to scroll to the number. Her thumb hovered over the *call* button as she choked back vomity sobs trying to calm down enough to be understood in a conversation when she realized something. She hadn't checked the whole house to be sure she was indeed alone. If she called her mother now it was a certainty the police would become involved.

She would tell Beth to hang up and call the police, or she would call the police, or she'd have both of them do it. Her current situation would explode into a *big* deal once those calls were made, bringing the police and her mother speeding to the house. Beth pictured police charging in and running around yelling to each other as they cleared the four rooms one by one.

They would find her on the bathroom floor half naked and covered in puke, and she would be carried out the front door in time for her mother to be coming up the steps. Once the police ascertained there was no one in the house, Beth would have to explain the mess, the blood, and the vomit.

If her mother knew Beth couldn't last three days on her own without a major freak out she would make her move home immediately. The house would be sold regardless of Aunt Agnes's wishes or it would be locked up and left to rot. Beth would be subject to living with her mother for at least two years regardless of her age.

She could see the entire scenario unfold in her mind, which is why she put the phone back on the sink, pulled herself up, and wiped her legs and arms off with a towel. She'd found the courage to walk the house and check all the closets, under the bed, and begrudgingly, the study. She even checked behind the bookshelves despite the gap between them and the wall being impossible for anyone to fit behind. The only place Beth didn't check was the basement. The closest she got was looking to see the door was still closed, but she didn't try the knob. She wasn't ready yet.

It didn't take long for her to check the rest of the house and, just as she thought, there was no one there. She knew she'd done the right thing not calling her mother and was proud for exercising restraint against the impulse to do what equated to throwing in the towel.

She set to work bandaging her foot tightly after slathering it in disinfectant. The wound didn't look that bad once it was cleaned out, so she decided to wait and see what it looked like after a day to assess whether she should seek medical attention.

She didn't make the call then, and she wouldn't make it now.

Beth pushed the phone back into her pocket, unfolded the paper bag, and stepped over to the mangled bird. As quickly as she could, Beth bent down, picked the bird up by its broken wing, and dropped it in the bag, unable to stifle a shiver as she did.

A squawk sounded behind her, and Beth whirled around, startled, scanning the yard for its origin. It was the first sign of wildlife she'd encountered outside of the dead bird in the bag at her feet. The squawk came again a second later, and Beth was able to zero in on it instantly. There were two more blackbirds perched on the lowest branch of one of the trees along the back edge of the yard, and they stared as if Beth was to blame for what happened to their friend.

A strong breeze blew across the yard, rustling the limb they were perched on, and one of the birds squawked again before they both disappeared into the forest. Something soft tickled across the top of Beth's bare, uninjured foot, and she looked down to see the feathers from the dead bird had been blown away except for the largest of the bunch. It kissed the top of Beth's foot before becoming stuck in the cuff of her pant leg.

She bent down and picked it up. The feather was so black it looked blue when she held it up in the waning sunlight. She picked up the paper bag and walked it to a metal trashcan on the side of the house. She glanced over her shoulder before dropping the bag in, half expecting to see the two blackbirds perched on the branch, but they were still gone.

She dropped the bag into the trashcan, replaced the lid, and went back inside. She didn't realize she was still holding the feather until she was standing in the kitchen.

THIRTEEN

BETH NEVER HAD MANY FRIENDS in school for a number of reasons. High school was her true first taste of the nonsensical class system she would be thrust into, on a much larger scale, of course, in four short years. Everything quickly turns political as kids splinter off into groups and cliques mostly having to do with what extracurricular aspect they were involved in, like sports, band, or theater.

Beth simply refused to fall into that line of thinking and remained somewhat of a loner or an outcast, depending on which social circle you asked. She had two or three friends along the way she would consider close, but after graduation they faded from her life after leaving town for big time universities in states far away.

She never had any problem with dating and seemed to perpetually have a boyfriend, each lasting only a few months like all good high school relationships. Beth may have been dubbed an outcast loner, but she'd grown into an undeniably attractive young woman. Despite the dyed black hair, black lipstick, and constant rotation of piercings and metal band t-shirts Beth's beauty showed through. This gave boys reason to stray from their chosen social circle to pursue her.

She remained unaffected by the lack of close companionship, preferring to read and listen to music very loudly and alone. This was a point her mother brought up during their many discussions around her moving out. She was concerned that, left to her own devices, Beth would become a shut in who had her groceries delivered and collected cats.

She couldn't contest her mother's point because it was a legitimate concern, but she did put her mind at ease by talking about getting a job. In a new environment she was bound to make friends with people she could spend time with. The response did little to assuage her mother's concerns, but it was enough to move the conversation along.

Beth stood in the kitchen watching the long, dark shadow of the trees fall across the backyard while silently wishing she *did* have a friend to call. Someone she could talk to and have a drink or two with, someone willing to explore the basement with her. After scrolling through the contacts in her phone so many times, she realized the only current number she had belonged to her mother. She wasn't even sure if most of the others still lived in state, let alone the town.

Her mother told her to stay out of the basement, but she didn't yet know what happened that morning, and Beth was reluctant to tell her. The door had been stuck shut the day before; she watched her mother struggle with it, and yet in the morning it stood open half an inch.

Beth was going to have to explore the basement on her own, but not until morning. She did not want to be in that basement alone at night no matter how much she told herself there was nothing to be afraid of. Besides, she'd had enough excitement for one day. Her foot still hurt but the pain had subsided significantly, and Beth limped out of the kitchen with her head down to avoid looking at the basement door.

She hadn't tried the door since she'd fallen against it, but that was another thing she'd worry about in the morning. At the moment, she was unwilling to dedicate any mindshare to the issue. Beth spun the large black feather between her thumb and forefinger as she stepped into the study to find something to read.

She'd searched the room thoroughly twice and found nothing out of the ordinary, but she was still wary of what she thought she'd seen hiding in the shadows. Her eyes trailed from the bookshelf, across the wall, and past the window to the desk. She didn't know why she was kidding herself. She knew she'd come for the journals.

Beth stepped over to the desk and sat down. She pulled her chair in close and placed the feather down next to the small lamp before tugging its short, tarnished chain. Soft yellow light from a flickering old bulb pooled in the center of the desk, and while faint, it was acceptable for reading.

She placed the journal from the night before down in front of her and opened to the picture of the woman burning in the fire. Beth thought if she found similar drawings in other journals she might be able to find what, if any, significance it held. The task would take time, but she was satisfied to have something to occupy her mind and keep it off the basement.

"Tomorrow," she said to herself. "Tomorrow I'm going down there and that will be that."

Her tone mimicked that of a mother telling her child to wait until Christmas morning to open their presents despite the lack of excitement she felt regarding the task. She'd made up her mind though, and nothing short of having to take the door off the hinges was going to stop her from exploring the basement to quell her fears.

Beth pulled another journal from the row and opened it to a random page. In the center was another drawing of the woman in the fire, but she was floating in the center of the flames now while three silhouetted figures stood before her holding hands. Beneath the drawing were the first words she'd come across that were in English.

Birth, Restoration, Power

Beth spent three hours poring over every page of that particular journal, trying to glean any decipherable information regarding or related to the woman in the fire, as well as any other words she could read. The closest thing she found was similar but still cryptic. It was a drawing of what appeared to be two distinctly different hands with their fingers knitted together in a fleshy cross-stitch. There were flames coming off the hands, but there was nothing written on the page.

When she could no longer fight the weight pulling her eyelids down, Beth used the blackbird's feather to mark her place. She left it on the desk next to the one she was using for reference and turned the lamp off.

That night Beth dreamt she was flying through the air above a lush forest that spread out in all directions as far as she could see. She felt no fear or anxiety as she sailed over trees, sometimes dipping close enough to touch leaves on the highest branches. It felt like her flight would last forever, and she wouldn't have minded if it did.

She saw a clearing up ahead and rode a jet stream toward it to investigate. The closer she got to the treetops, the more speed she picked up, which was especially exhilarating until Beth realized she couldn't slow down, nor was she able to change direction. As she skidded across the treetops at breakneck speed she could see the roof of a house peeking through the branches.

When she reached the clearing she couldn't stop herself from swooping down into it. She was going so fast it barely registered when she saw herself standing in the kitchen through the window she was quickly approaching.

Just before she hit the glass Beth saw the blackbird reflected back at her.

———

Beth was halfway through another journal before the rumbling in her stomach became too much of a distraction. She'd been up for two and a half hours drinking coffee, but she'd yet to eat something. The dream shocked her awake well before the sun had come up, and the lingering adrenaline would not let her go back to sleep.

She got up and made her way to the study to continue looking through her aunt's journals for clues as to the meaning of the drawings or anything else that seemed interesting but found nothing useful. The only words she'd found in English were the ones below the woman in the fire.

Birth, Restoration, Power

Although Beth had no context or frame of reference for what those words meant she couldn't help but feel something ominous attached to them.

Her stomach gurgled and cramped, begging for anything but more caffeine, so she marked her place with the feather, pushed away from the desk, and stood to stretch. Her back popped and cracked like thin ice on a frozen pond breaking apart in the warming sunlight.

She had a few pieces of bread, peanut butter, and a box of granola bars left, but a trip to the store was inevitable. Beth stepped lightly on bare feet down the short hallway to the kitchen, being careful not to put too much weight on her injured foot. She was still in panties and her regular sleep shirt, which was emblazoned with a very faded Misfits logo of the Crimson Ghost. She found it at a thrift store and bought it despite the size being 2XL. It was too cool to pass up, and she'd been sleeping in it ever since.

Beth needed to shower, but decided it could wait until after she ate some peanut butter toast. Her stomach grumbled in agreement, begging for something solid to soak up the caffeine in her system. Upon entering the kitchen, Beth kept her head down until she was at the counter by the sink. She plugged in the toaster, took a deep breath, and whirled around quickly to face the basement door.

The knot in her stomach loosened when she saw the door remained closed. She didn't want to see it when she first walked past, afraid of being forced to face her fear if it happened to be open again.

The door was to the right of the kitchen entrance, and if it *were* open Beth would have been forced to investigate right then and there. Since it was closed she could take her time working up the courage to investigate.

Beth dropped two of the last five pieces of bread she had into the toaster and pressed the button to engage the heated coils within. Her gaze drifted out the window and across the yard where she saw two blackbirds perched on a low branch. They were blackbirds, yes, but whether they were the same ones she'd seen while disposing of their dead friend was not very likely. At least that's what she told herself.

The toast popped up at the same time a loud knock came from the front door. Beth screamed. The blackbirds scattered.

FOURTEEN

"I'M NOT SAYING I DON'T appreciate it, Mom, I'm just saying at least give me a courtesy text if you're on the way. What if I was . . .?"

Beth struggled to come up with something inappropriate she could have been doing that might be considered off-putting to her mother. Five years ago her mother walked in on her losing her virginity to Russ Sanders and simply backed out and closed the door without saying a word.

Exactly ninety seconds later Russ tore down the stairs with Beth close behind. He muttered a quick goodbye before rushing out the door, slamming it behind him. Beth cinched her robe and trudged into the kitchen, startled to find her mother sitting at the table.

"Cheer up, sweetheart, it gets better," her mother said with a sly smile. "They won't all be *minute men*."

A second later both women were laughing, and Beth's mother went to the freezer to retrieve a pint of birthday cake-flavored ice cream. The two sat at the table eating from the carton while Beth's mother told the story of how she lost her virginity and how awkward of an experience it was.

She didn't shame Beth or make her feel like she'd done something wrong and instead comforted her by relating. Her mother never made her feel uncomfortable about sex, drugs, or any of the other typical topics that triggered unease between parent and child.

"Well, I was up early and went to the store," she replied. "The groceries were already in the car, and I figured it made more sense to bring them straight here instead of unpacking them at home, then repacking them after I'd obtained permission to visit you."

Beth's mother had been the one who knocked on the door. She knocked hard because she was losing her grip on the bags she was carrying and wanted to communicate urgency through the intensity of her blows. As if she were able to sense Beth was running short of 'rations,' her mother swooped in with enough food to keep her stocked up for at least two and half weeks.

The coincidence would seem eerie if Beth weren't used to her mother pulling stunts like this her whole life. She had a habit of showing up places when Beth needed something she just so happened to have with her. At this point she expected it to happen, which is why this particular instance came as no surprise.

"Don't be dramatic," Beth replied, dropping the annoyance from her voice. "You know you don't need permission, and you *know* I appreciate it, but I need to have a chance to figure this stuff out on my own."

"I know, I know," her mother said, moving cans of tomato soup and green beans from a bag on the counter into one of the cabinets. "But you have your whole life to learn how to grocery shop. You can let your mother spoil you every once in a while."

Beth knew her mom was being sincere despite the sarcastic delivery, so she decided to stop harping on it. Also, the groceries allowed Beth to hang on to the finite amount of money she had, allowing a bit more of a time-cushion before finding a job would be necessary. She stepped lightly across the kitchen to her mother, minding her ailing foot, and helped put the last of the cans in the cabinet.

"Thank you," Beth said wrapping her arms around her.

"Of course, dear," she replied, reciprocating the hug.

They pulled away and both women fought back tears they didn't want the other to see. Beth's mother looked down and her smile quickly faded.

"What the hell happened to your foot? You didn't go into the basement, did you?"

She gripped Beth by the shoulders and shot a look in the direction of the basement door. Beth had completely forgotten about her foot and looked down to see crimson blooms spreading across the bandage. She must have stepped wrong and reopened the cut without realizing. It struck Beth as odd her mother immediately assumed her injury had something to do with the basement.

"Oh, I stepped on a piece of glass from a mug I broke. I think it's okay though."

She looked up to meet her mother's eyes, but her gaze was aimed at the basement door. Beth contemplated telling her mother about the basement door being open, the bird, the dreams, the horror she'd glimpsed hiding in the shadows of the bookcase, all of it. She lost her nerve upon seeing the concern in her mother's eyes.

Or was it fear?

"Why did you think it had something to do with the basement?" Beth phrased the question in her head, but never meant to audibly manifest it.

"Well, I . . ." She whipped her head back quickly toward the door again, stealing a final glance before continuing. "I just thought . . . the stairs. There could have been an exposed nail or something even worse."

"What is it about th—"

"Your foot!"

Her mother gestured empathically down at the puddle of blood growing beneath her daughter's foot.

———————

Beth sat on the toilet with the lid closed while her mother knelt to finish rewrapping the injured foot. This was after she'd washed and rinsed it four different times with scalding water under the faucet in the tub. She'd left Beth in the bathroom alone for a minute and come back with two items she'd retrieved from her purse.

One was a small, translucent, cylindrical bottle with no markings on it, similar to what someone would transfer a liquid product to in order to board a plane with it. She thought the limit might be two and half ounces, but they changed things like that all the time. Inside the bottle was what her mother referred to as a *special* disinfectant soap. The other item was a tube of superglue.

She washed the wound again, using the special, oily soap and dried it thoroughly before pulling the cap off the superglue and squeezing a cylinder of the off-white adhesive across the length of the cut. Beth winced from the sting that accompanied filling the gap between her torn flesh with a foreign substance. She had heard of deep cuts being superglued together in lieu of stitches but thought it was something only done in the movies.

Growing up, Beth's mother used all kinds of unusual home remedies on her daughter's scrapes, scratches, and even rashes, allergic or otherwise. Many of them involved homemade concoctions, and Beth assumed this was something all mothers did.

She was nine years old before she'd even seen a tube of Neosporin at a friend's house, and her stomach soured at the sight of the substance being administered. There was a strange coldness in watching her friend Sara squeeze out an enormous glob from the small yellow tube directly onto the unwashed, bleeding abrasion she'd acquired on her elbow.

The two had been taking turns riding Sara's new scooter up and down the street, and with each trip their confidence grew. With their newfound courage the girls started to go faster and even attempted mini bunny-hops into the driveway, pulling up on the handlebars as the front tire reached a small incline.

This went on without incident until Sarah lost her grip after mistiming a jump. The scooter flew out from under her, and while she landed on her feet at first, the momentum pushed her down on her rear-end. Her left elbow dragged across the cement, resulting in the injury Beth had watched Sara tend to.

The girl didn't bother rubbing in the store-bought healing ointment before slapping a Hello Kitty-themed adhesive bandage over it and announcing she was ready to go back out and try again.

When she went home Beth told her mother all about it and asked why their medicine didn't come in a colorful tube with a futuristic sounding name?

"That's just how some people do things," her mother told her. "*We* don't do things that way."

Her mother's explanation was dry, matter-of-fact, and abrupt, just as Beth had come to expect, and she accepted it without question. It was clear Beth's mother didn't make her own superglue, but she'd been using more and more store-bought items in combination with her own concoctions lately.

After the appropriate amount of glue had been squeezed into the cut, Beth's mother used the rest of the gauze in the first-aid kit to wrap her foot. It was much tighter than when Beth had wrapped it herself, and she flinched against the pressure.

"It has to be tight," her mother said before Beth could vocalize her discomfort. "Once the glue has some time to set we'll loosen it, but we don't want the cut to open up again."

"Jeez, it's cutting off my circulation," Beth said, "and I thought superglue was supposed to set immediately?"

Her mother stood up, collected her small bottle of homemade soap in one hand and the tube of superglue in the other without replying to her daughter's question. The woman glanced in the mirror, made a small adjustment to her hair, and walked out the bathroom door without saying a word.

———

"When did you clean up the blood?" Beth said.

Beth was sitting at the small, round table in the kitchen rattling the ice in a glass of water while her mother was across the kitchen at the stove hard-boiling a pot of eggs. She was going to make egg salad with half of them and leave the other half for Beth to eat throughout the week.

"What was that?" Her mother kept her back to Beth when she answered, giving the majority of her focus to the boiling pot in front of her.

"The blood," Beth repeated. "The blood from my foot."

"Oh, I cleaned that up while you were still in the bathroom."

Her mother turned the burner off as she lifted the pot and shuffled down the counter to the sink. Steam rose like conjured spirits escaping the void as the scalding water met the sink's cold steel.

"Oh," Beth said, not quite ready to let it go, "but you were in the living room putting your things back into your purse."

"Well, of course I cleaned it before I went to put my things away," she answered, glancing back over her shoulder as the last of the water escaped down the drain with a dying hiss. "I couldn't just leave blood on the floor like that. Now would you mind giving me a hand?"

"Sure."

Beth rose from the table and crossed the kitchen to meet her mother at the sink.

"I think there's a mixing bowl in the cabinet over there," her mother said, pointing. "Can you get it down for me, please?"

The bowl was right where she said it would be, and Beth took it down and handed it to her. She stared absently out the window while her mother put half of the eggs in the bowl and slid back down the counter to peel and prep. Beth's eyes wandered to the spot where the blackbird had hit the glass, and in this light she could still see the smudge left from the eyeball's impact.

She refocused her eyes to look through the glass and noticed something odd and off-putting about the trees. She'd dismissed it earlier as a trick of the light, an illusion caused by the sun's position in the sky. She couldn't use the same explanation on herself again this time because the change was too obvious.

The trees were getting closer to the house.

Her mother stayed for two more hours after they'd eaten, and Beth helped her clean up the kitchen from the meal. She couldn't help glancing at the basement door while the two engaged in small talk. Her mother did the same thing, stealing looks over her shoulder when Beth was distracted with putting away dishes.

Beth wanted to ask her mother about the drawing of the woman in the fire from the journal, and she almost brought it up several times but thought better of it. She wasn't sure how to talk about the subject without causing her mother to find reason to worry. Plus, there was a chance if Beth brought it up now her mother would simply pack up the journals, take them home, and that would be that.

She wanted to do more research on her own before talking to her mother and suddenly found herself anxious to get back to it.

Whatever was in the basement could wait a little while longer while she indulged in this task.

Birth, Restoration, Power

Those words stuck in Beth's head, and she was compelled to know what they meant, desperately, in fact. She was certain the answer was within one of those journals.

"Okay, it's getting late," her mother said, hanging a dishtowel over the faucet to dry. "I'm heading home, but I want you to keep that bandage on your foot for a full twenty-four hours, understand? Take it off tomorrow afternoon, wash it again, and let me know if the cut opens back up."

"Okay, Mom," she said in a mocking, child-like tone.

"I'm serious," her mother said, collecting her purse from the couch on her way to the door. "It could get infected, and then you'd really be in some pain."

"I know," Beth said in her normal voice. "I'll take good care of it and let you know if anything changes."

Beth's mother opened the front door and turned around to embrace her daughter.

"I love you," she said.

"I love you too," Beth said, "and seriously, thank you for everything."

Beth's mother smiled, nodded, and closed the door behind her.

FIFTEEN

BEFORE BETH GOT BACK TO looking over the journals
there was one thing she wanted to do. She dug through a pile of
clothes until she found the pair of fluorescent, lime-green socks she
was looking for and took one of them with her through the kitchen
and out the back door.

On her way to the edge of the yard Beth bent over and picked
up a thin piece of broken tree limb that was most likely a result of
the storm on the first night. It was a little more than a foot long and
hadn't gone brittle yet.

When she reached the tree line Beth tied the sock to the stick
before plunging it into the ground beside the closest trees. She was
certain she was imagining them getting closer to the house, but if
Beth ever doubted herself she could check the marker to put her
mind at ease.

She paused and looked back to the house as a breeze cooler than
normal for this time of year blew through, violently whipping her
hair across her face. Goosebumps raced up her arms, and she reflexively crossed them to combat the chill. The lime-green sock
whipped and flapped in the sudden gust, but the knot kept it firmly

attached to the stick.

Beth began to make her way back to the house, her arms hugged tightly against her chest. She was halfway there when a piercing squawk slashed the early evening quiet to ribbons. Anticipating a dive bomb attack from the blackbirds, Beth dropped to the ground and covered her head with her arms. She screamed but the sound stuck in her throat when she fell, manifesting instead as an inaudible croak.

She lay with her face pressed against the grass, eyes shut tight and arms wrapped around her head and neck for twenty seconds before relaxing her guard, albeit slowly. Beth rose carefully and kept her head on a swivel, looking for a sneak attack that never came.

The sound of rushing rapids ripped through the woods, past the trees, and into Beth's face as the chilled breeze came harder this time. The wind smacked her face like it was trying to jam tiny icicles into each pore. She turned away from the woods and ran back into the house, slamming the backdoor behind her.

She was in such a hurry to get back inside she didn't notice the stick with the sock was now six inches behind the tree she'd lined it up with.

SIXTEEN

BETH SAT HUNCHED OVER THE desk in the study with four open journals in front of her. She'd been there since coming in from the backyard after placing her makeshift marker at the tree line. She'd written off hearing the bird to it being the wind, her imagination, or a little bit of both.

She was shaking when she'd come back inside and descended immediately upon the journals in an attempt to calm herself by way of distraction. Now, three hours later, she'd yet to find anything written in English but still meticulously pored over pages, looking for any perceived connection to the woman in the fire.

A thought occurred to Beth as she stood, giving her legs a much needed stretch. Aunt Agnes wasn't just curious about the occult. Her interest went far beyond hobbyist. Her aunt was a witch, wasn't she?

Beth decided it was time for a break that included a little more of the wine her mother brought, or maybe a lot more. She stretched and her stomach emitted a soft rumble to remind her she should have some food with her wine.

When the water first reached her toes Beth mistook it for the sensation of blood returning to her sleeping foot. It only took a second to recognize this was not the familiar pins and needles of a post-sleep limb; Beth was standing in a puddle of water. Again.

Had the pipe come loose, allowing the contents of the sink to spill out from the cabinet, across the floor, and down the hall? It would make sense except there was no water in the sink this time, and there hadn't been for hours.

She thought maybe the pipe that fed water to the faucet had burst, which meant this small puddle had the potential to get much worse. She leapt into action, having the sudden thought flash through her mind of water pouring out of the front of the house, destroying furniture along the way while ruining the floor completely.

Beth stepped lightly through the water out to the hall, turned toward the kitchen, and froze.

It took a second, maybe two, to fully process what she was seeing. Her brain rejected the possibility of it actually being real, but after her eyes resubmitted their claim all doubt was erased. Beth thought it might be the thing she saw hiding in the shadows of the study, but it was too dark to see anything but a silhouette.

Seven feet of hallway separated Beth from what was standing in the entrance to the kitchen, its shoulders rising and falling rhythmically with each breath. The basement door was standing wide open to the left of the thing, leaving no confusion as to where it came from.

The in and out rush of Beth's short, shallow breaths pounded in her head, resonating like an orchestral percussion section. Her eyes followed the trail of water down the hall where it pooled at the thing's feet. Who or what ever this was, they were drenched, and what Beth hoped was only water fell from its hands and arms in long, steady drips.

The shock paralyzed her in place until the thing lunged, clearing the space between them in a single leap. Beth's limbs unlocked and she spun on her heel to sprint for the door behind her, but she didn't make it far. The front door was gone, and so were the couch, the living room, and the house itself.

In their place were trees and fire.

The journal closest to the edge of the desk fell when Beth jerked awake, and it landed awkwardly open and facedown, bending pages in on themselves. The light coming through the window allowed Beth to see she was still at the desk in her aunt's study. She hadn't confronted a shadowy, wet creature from the basement, and the forest hadn't replaced the front half of the house. She'd had another nightmare, which had become all too frequent since moving into the house.

Beth stood up and stretched her legs before bending to retrieve the fallen journal. She smoothed the bent pages but refrained from flipping through the book again. She needed a break and didn't want to inadvertently be sucked back in if something interesting caught her eye. She pulled the chain on the lamp and stepped to the door when a sudden wave of déjà vu stopped her in her tracks.

Since she moved into the house her sleep had been plagued by nightmares that felt terrifyingly real.

She limped out into the hall to find it free of dark and drippy creatures, but more importantly, the basement door was still shut. With each step she became more aware of the superglue cinching together her bisected flesh, and the sensation mimicked what Beth imagined having a hole through your foot would feel like.

She crossed the hall to her bedroom, and beelined it for the bathroom to alleviate the sudden and painful pressure of her full bladder. Beth sat on the toilet and thought about her experiences over the last few days, having wished she'd talked to her mom instead of being concerned with appearing immature or not ready to live on her own.

Considering the last few days, Beth was starting to think maybe she *wasn't* ready. The basement door, the bird hitting the window, seeing sinister beings hiding in the shadows of the study were all just things that happened.

There was no reason for her to believe these instances were related, but perhaps she'd subconsciously linked them together, thereby creeping herself out. Maybe she always knew she wasn't ready to be on her own but refused to let herself believe it?

She didn't realize she'd started to cry until a tear landed softly on her thigh. It stuck for a moment before sluggishly sliding down the inside of her leg and into the water below. She wiped her eyes on the back of her hand, got up, and stepped over to the shower.

She turned the water on and shed her sleep shirt, tossing it on the floor behind her. She was stronger than this, and she knew it. She *was* ready to be on her own and bad dreams along with perceived coincidences weren't going to convince her otherwise. Steam was rolling off the water when Beth stepped beneath it, and she washed her face, defiantly erasing the unwelcome tears.

She could feel her confidence returning when she was struck by another thought. What if she was wrong? What if the dreams and the basement and the bird were signals that something terrible was coming? Was it possible she hadn't imagined the pale yellow eyes and sharply twisted grin hiding in the shadows of the study?

Beth lathered and rinsed and then lathered again, trying to collect her thoughts. Was the house creepy because creepy things were happening, or was it creepy because it was someplace different than she was used to?

Another sudden thought occurred to Beth, and she thrust her

head beneath the water and rubbed vigorously to get the soap out of her hair. Satisfied, she turned the water off and hurriedly stepped out of the shower. Small patches of foamy bubbles dotted random sections and stood out against her coal-black hair, which would require more rinsing to be rid of them completely.

Beth quickly ran a towel across most of her body before abandoning it to the floor as she crossed into her bedroom with frantic urgency, looking for something she could throw on fast. While washing her hair for the third time, Beth realized there was a way she could know for sure if it was all in her head.

She was going to check the stick with the sock tied to it.

Beth put on a pair of black workout shorts and pulled an Electric Wizard t-shirt over her head sans bra as she hurried into the hallway, trying not to put too much weight on her injured foot. There would be time for proper undergarments *after* she checked the stick. She stepped into the kitchen without breaking stride, her eyes leveled at the backdoor. She didn't look at the basement when she rushed by, but the close proximity was enough to make her shiver.

Beth blew through the backdoor, not bothering to shut it behind her. In that moment there was nothing more important than checking if the marker still lined up with the trees. She dropped five hard steps across the grass but stopped cold, tipping forward from the momentum, almost losing her balance. She didn't realize she'd been holding her breath until she heard herself exhale many seconds later.

She could see the stick with the sock from where she stood. It was at least fifteen feet behind a wall of trees that had advanced halfway across the backyard. She stared through the small gaps between the trees at the sock as it flopped gracelessly in the sharp, cold breeze as it began to pick up. She blinked hard, expecting to see the trees back where they belonged, but there was no such luck.

Beth wasn't sure if she should try to squeeze past the trees to take a closer look at her marker or turn and run into the house with no plan beyond that. A second later her decision was made when the piercing squawk of blackbirds sounded from deep within the encroaching forest. Beth turned and sprinted back to the house, slamming the backdoor behind her.

She spun around, turned the deadbolt into place, and crouched beneath the window on the upper half of the door. She rose slowly so she was able to see through the pane. Beth had no idea why she was hiding or what she was even hiding from. She didn't know why she bothered to lock the door, as if a four-inch piece of steel stuck in a wooden hole could keep out a forest of advancing trees.

Beth hoped she was experiencing one of those dream within a dream sequences like in the movies, which was hacky nowadays but she fell for it every time. This was no dream though, and she knew she wasn't about to wake up safe in her bed.

She got up close to the glass to take a better look at the entire yard when three blackbirds crashed against the glass in quick succession, sounding like the triple report of a high-powered rifle. A nearly imperceptible echo decayed quickly in the small space of the kitchen.

Beth shrieked and jumped away from the door, holding her hands over her ears. She knew she was screaming this time because she could feel her vocal cords vibrating in her throat, stretching and tearing from the misuse of not using her diaphragm. She had been in theater briefly in high school, so she knew how to project to the back of the room, but proper breathing technique was the last thing on her mind at the moment.

Beth went to scream again but decided not to waste energy on something unrelated to her getting out of the house. If this was truly what living on your own was like, Beth could easily admit she wasn't ready and would gladly move back in with her mom for the rest of her life.

She took her hands away from her head and looked up at the glass. It didn't break, but the outside was now streaked translucent red and dark yellow from the birds' heads cracking open on impact. A single black feather stuck to the pane and slid slowly down the glass, riding a stream of brain-flecked blood.

Beth jumped to her feet, turned, and crossed the kitchen, pretending she didn't hear what sounded like someone or something pounding its way up the basement steps. What she couldn't pretend was not to see the figure in the study as she dashed down the hall to the front door.

There was no trick being played by shadow and light conspiring together to break Beth's sanity through a combined creation of fear. She wasn't asleep and dreaming, and she was completely sober.

There was no denying it now.

SEVENTEEN

THE THING STANDING IN THE study resembled something human in that it stood on two legs, but the similarities ended there. Its skin was black, shriveled, and scarred all over, an obvious result of being badly burned. In her passing glance Beth could make out bulbous, low-hanging breasts seared to the flesh of the thing's bowling ball-sized potbelly.

It was the face, though. It was the same face she told herself she'd imagined, only now there were no shadows to obscure it. It was the face that propelled Beth to keep going, to get out of the house, get in her car, and drive as far away as possible.

The face was charcoal-colored, its features twisted and distorted by deep, winding grooves made from melted skin and scar tissue. Its nose was thin, pointed at the end, and smashed up between two squinted yellow eyes as if added to its face as an afterthought.

A crooked, lipless mouth split the burned flesh horizontally across the thing's head, running from one flat, shapeless ear to the other. Its teeth were a much deeper yellow than the eyes and appeared hastily cobbled into the creature's wide smile. None of them were the same size or in the correct place in the mouth. It was like the thing had ripped the sharpest teeth from the jawbones of various carnivorous animals and forced them into its toothless, rotting gums.

Beth passed the open door too quickly to take in every detail of the creature, but what she did see was terrifying enough. Long, thick strands of drool dripped from its horribly misshapen maw and pooled on the floor around shriveled and charred feet. Black flecks of burned skin dotted the drool-puddle like lily pads in a swamp, but these were details Beth didn't see.

She practically fell into the front door but was able to keep her balance by grabbing the doorknob. Beth flung the door open and heard it slam against the wall inside as she leapt down the porch steps. She hit the ground and broke into a sprint, making a beeline for her Cherokee, unconcerned for her cut foot.

She was only vaguely aware the sharp stones in the dirt driveway were tearing into the bandage, aggravating the wound. Her other foot incurred many small punctures from the rocks, and she could feel the blood pushing out from the tiny tears with each step.

When she reached the Jeep she was shaking so hard she needed to hold the door handle with both hands to get a grip. She jumped into the car and slammed the door, locking it instantly.

Her eyes fell down to the keys dangling from the ignition as if she'd left them there yesterday on purpose, knowing her future self would need them. Without hesitation she turned the key, put the Cherokee in drive, and hit the gas while pulling a hard right turn toward the gap in the trees split by the driveway that led down to the road.

The Jeep's spinning rear wheels kicked up a cloud of dust and fired rocks off in the direction of the porch. Centrifugal force pushed Beth's body into the turn, and she hoped she could make the quick change in navigation without flipping the vehicle over.

Her mother constantly reminded Beth of how easy it was for Jeeps to flip over, especially during the first month she had it. Her mother's nagging was annoying but effective because every time she approached a turn she could hear her mother in the back of her head screaming accident statistics.

Beth was always careful to slow down more than necessary before turning and never made any evasive moves like the one she was currently trying to pull off. The back end of the Jeep started to fishtail, and she gripped the steering wheel tightly, trying to keep it from being jerked out of her hand. She felt the top-heavy vehicle begin to lean and slammed on the brakes, not knowing what else to do.

She closed her eyes and clenched her teeth as she felt the vehicle begin to spin out. The vehicle's direction changed violently back and forth while Beth held the wheel tight like a captain steering his ship through a churning, angry sea. The Jeep lurched to a stop, remaining in the upright position, and Beth opened her eyes to find her view obscured by the dust cloud she'd kicked up.

The erratic shift in motion had thrown off her equilibrium, and she struggled to see through the slow settling dust for the opening of the driveway. Two eternally long seconds later Beth saw she was facing away from the house in the direction of her exit.

She pressed on the gas but not too hard this time so as to avoid fishtailing. She was closing the fifteen-foot patch of gravel between her and the exit and began to slowly accelerate. Beth's eyes went wide with disbelief, and she pressed the brake with both feet, stopping inches from the opening.

Something was wrong.

"No," Beth said, throwing the Cherokee into park before pushing her way out the driver side door. "No, no, no!"

She repeated the word as she stumbled to the front of the vehicle to confirm what she saw from behind the wheel. The trees lining the driveway had moved in toward each other by more than two feet on each side. The path was now far too narrow for the Jeep to fit through.

Beth stood next to her car, taking deep breaths, trying to calm down enough to think even though she was close to having a total breakdown. She contemplated running down the sloping narrow driveway, but it was full of the same jagged rocks she'd walked over while hurrying to the car.

She could tolerate cutting up the bottom of her good foot while aggravating her existing wound when she ran from the porch to the Jeep, but walking down the steep, craggy-rocked, hundred and fifty foot driveway was a different story.

The stinging from the bottom of her feet had begun to cut through the adrenaline in Beth's system, giving her a tame taste of the awful pain yet to come. In times like this, when your life was in danger, Beth learned an inborn fight or flight reaction was supposed to take hold and override all other thoughts in the interest of preserving life.

If she were in a movie she could see her character sprinting headlong down the driveway with no regard for her injured feet, which would allow her to escape without being impeded by pain. This wasn't a movie though, and the intensifying irritation in her feet relayed the message to her brain that trying to run, or even walk slowly, down the driveway was not going to work out. Still, Beth took a shaky step past the front end of the Cherokee to begin what would no doubt be a long and painful journey to the road below.

The instant her foot touched down a scream came ripping up the hill. It sounded like three octaves of tone layered on top of each other with the dry, abrasive quality of an old, badly scratched vinyl record. This wasn't the scream of a retreating victim; it was the foreboding wail of an approaching predator.

The trees on either side of her shook, and the scream came through the woods again, only closer this time. Beth leapt back from the driveway and walked backward with her hand on the side of the Cherokee to guide her. Now all of the trees surrounding the house were shaking, and Beth glanced over her shoulder to see the front door still standing open.

She had expected someone or something to follow her out like last time, but so far that wasn't the case. Through the open door Beth could see all the way through the living room to the hall. It appeared clear, but the possibility of a sneak attack from either side was a definite possibility.

She was damned either way she went but felt she had a better chance, albeit slim, at surviving in the house instead of out in the vibrating, ever-constricting woods. The hellish cry of what waited for her outside came again with a guttural, unholy shriek, solidifying the decision. Beth turned and limped back to the house as quickly as her wounded feet could take her.

Beth took one more look behind her as she stepped up onto the porch. The opening to the driveway was gone, now replaced by trees like it had never been there. The front end of her Jeep was inches from the encroaching trees, and Beth briefly wondered what would become of the vehicle if they came any closer.

The thought was fleeting and forgotten as she turned back to the open front door, preparing for what may or may not be waiting inside. An image of burned, flaking flesh and jagged yellow teeth flashed in her mind as she stepped across the threshold into the house.

Beth was at least mentally prepared to face the thing in the study or a creature from the basement, but she was in no way prepared for what was waiting in her living room.

"Mom?"

Her mother was standing beside the couch, but that didn't make sense. Beth's head hurt trying to process what was surely a fear-induced hallucination. She didn't realize she'd shut the door behind her until the sound of it slamming startled her. Beth looked over her shoulder at the door for half a second, fully expecting the living room to be empty when she turned back around, but her mother was still there.

"Beth," her mother said calmly, holding out her hands. "Beth, it's okay. It really is me, so calm down. I'm really here."

"But . . . wait," Beth stammered, unable to process so much at once. First the trees were trying to keep her from leaving, and now her mother had somehow appeared out of thin air. "How is this . . . What is happening?"

She was numbed by fear and confusion, not realizing how much colder it was in the house now. Her mother stepped toward her slowly, hands out, arms extended, doing her best to put her daughter at ease.

"It's okay, Beth. It's okay, baby."

Her mother's voice was soft and comforting. It cleaved through the insanity surrounding Beth, and she latched on to it like the life preserver she desperately needed to pull her from the dark, choppy water she'd fallen into. Her mother took another slow step forward and maintained eye contact while continuing to whisper reassurances.

Beth took a step toward her mother, locking onto the signal she needed to guide her to safety. She fell into her mother's arms and shook with sobs, unable to communicate her appreciation vocally.

For a moment, as she cried against her mother's chest, Beth forgot about the trees, the basement, the birds, and whatever was waiting for her in the study. She forgot that only seconds ago she'd been running for her life from an unknown, possibly supernatural threat.

She forgot it was impossible for her mother to even be there with her.

The moment was short-lived as all of the unpleasantness temporarily expelled from her mind came crashing back down in one concussive realization. Beth pushed off her mother and took a step back, rubbing her eyes with her palms. She could feel her racing heartbeat through the throbbing cuts on her feet, but the cool hardwood floor was soothing and would be easier to traverse than the rocky driveway if she needed to make a break for it.

"What the fuck? Who are you even? You can't be my mom. That's not possible!"

"Sweetheart," her mother began. "I'm about to tell you a lot of things you aren't going to believe are possible, but I need you to trust me. I know you're freaked out."

"Freaked out? I am far beyond *freaked out* at this point! Did you know the trees are moving closer to the house, and there's some . . . *thing* in the study, and why is it so cold in here?"

Beth folded her arms across her chest and rubbed the gooseflesh sprouting on the back of her arms in an attempt to keep it from breaking out across her entire body. She glanced past her mother and saw a shadow pass across the light coming through the hallway. An inaudible gasp escaped Beth's parted lips, and she took another step back, her left heel inches from the front door.

"It's okay," her mother said, not bothering to look back at what caught her daughter's eye. "No one is going to hurt you. Please give me the chance to explain and you—"

"Who else is here?" Beth hadn't taken her eyes off the hallway since she'd glimpsed the shadow."

"I—"

"Who else is here?" Beth growled through clenched teeth.

Her arms were now at her sides, her hands balled tightly in tiny fists. Her mother's mouth was open but no words were coming out, like she'd suddenly become lost mid-thought.

Before she managed to respond to the question a shadow filled the hallway again, but this time it wasn't passing from one side to the other. The shadow grew long across the living room floor, signifying the attached owner was getting closer. A moment later, Beth's Aunt Agnes was standing there holding a tray with three mugs and a teakettle balanced on it.

"I think you better calm down and let your mother explain, dear."

EIGHTEEN

BETH SAT ON THE COUCH clutching the handle connected
to a mug of tea her dead aunt had given her. She kept her other arm
wrapped tightly across her stomach, using the free hand to pinch
her side every few seconds each time, hoping it would be the one to
wake her up.

Her mother sat beside her and angled in toward her very confused daughter. Aunt Agnes brought a chair in from the kitchen
table and sat next to the coffee table a few feet in front of Beth. So
far, Aunt Agnes hadn't done much talking with the majority of explanation coming from Beth's mother.

Beth couldn't look at either woman. She stared into the space
between them while words she was hearing rattled around inside her
head, unable to quite get where they needed to go in order to be
made sense of. Soon her mother's voice droned off deep into the
back of Beth's head where it became a steady buzz that doubled as a
soundtrack for the blank space blurring before her unblinking eyes.

She suddenly focused her eyes, and the mug fell from her hand,
missing her bare thigh, and it crashed down to the rug the couch sat
on.

"Beth!"

Her name. That's what had broken her from the trance she was falling into. Someone was calling her name.

"Are you listening to me? Are you all right?"

Beth looked down to see Aunt Agnes at her feet picking up pieces of the mug she'd dropped. It had broken into three large chunks instead of shattering on account of the rug breaking its fall.

"I'm—I'm sorry," Beth murmured, looking up from someone who was supposed to be dead back to someone who wasn't supposed to be there.

"Don't worry about it, dear," Aunt Agnes said as she stood up holding the broken pieces of mug. "This is a lot for you to take in all at once."

Take in? The truth was Beth hadn't retained a single thing her mother said to her. She was not presently firing on all cylinders after the shock of seeing her 'dead' aunt walk into the room, and she'd since been trying to kick-start her brain but the motor wasn't turning over.

Her mother was going to have to repeat most, if not all, of what she'd told Beth so far. As Aunt Agnes turned down the hall with the pieces of broken mug Beth noticed the light reflecting off a trail of moisture left behind from where her long dress dragged the floor. Her mother noticed Beth's wandering gaze and very gently rested a hand on her daughter's forearm.

"Beth," she said, softly rubbing the girl's arm.

When Beth was younger and sought her mother's comfort she would rub her arm the same way while saying whatever reassuring words pertained to the situation. There was no denying this was indeed her mother, but knowing this didn't make Beth feel any better.

"Beth," her mother repeated. "Honey, were you able to take any of that in?"

Feeling suddenly coherent, Beth turned to her mother, allowing her eyes to focus on the woman for the first time since she'd found her in the living room.

"Witches," Beth said. "You said something about witches. Are you two witches? Am . . . *I* a witch?"

Her mother sighed, her mouth pulled tightly in a straight line across her face.

Beth thought she heard the actual word 'witch' used, but she could have assumed based on the bits of context she retained. It could have been in her head. She also had a hazy recollection of her mother saying something about *tradition* and *ceremony* and—

"Restoration!" Beth blurted the word the instant it came into her head. It was one of the only three words she was able to read in the journals.

Birth. Restoration. Power.

Beth's mother blanched at the exclamation with an angry look but quickly relaxed the expression into a soft smile, attempting to mask her reaction.

"You *did* say that right? Restoration? I've been going through the journals, the ones in the study, and the only words in English I can find are birth, restoration, and power. They were written together. I haven't found them listed independently from one another."

"You're right. I did." Her mother's smile was now wide, toothy, overcompensating. "I did say restoration, and that is part of it. A big part, I might add."

"O-o-okay." Beth drew out the word, over-accentuating the look of anticipation on her face she used to communicate piqued interest to her mother. "So . . . what is *it*? What is restoration a big part of?"

"Well, The Cycle," her mother said as if Beth should already know exactly what she meant. "It's . . . there's a ceremony involved."

Beth knew she remembered hearing the word *ceremony* at some point in her mother's initial—and unintentionally ignored— explanation.

"Every twenty-three years," her mother continued, "there are certain astrological elements aligned in a very specific way and for a very short time. It's during this time your aunt and I perform the ceremony of The Cycle. It's what we've always done and always will do without exception."

"What does this have to do with me? Why do you need me to be here for you to do it?"

Footsteps coming down the hall signaled her aunt's return, and Beth turned to watch her enter. Aunt Agnes stepped into the living room, her dress now soaking wet. A puddle began to form around her feet where the saturated fabric touched the floor.

The woman's eyes had turned a dark-yellow color that popped against the burnt flesh of her face. Aunt Agnes opened her mouth in a mocking smile, displaying teeth Beth thought she'd only imagined. The thing that was Aunt Agnes gave a haughty huff before answering Beth's question.

"Haven't you figured it out yet, darling? We're going to kill you."

Beth didn't remember hitting her head, but the inside of her skull throbbed with the resonance of having been concussed. Her right knee seethed with pain like it had been set on fire and was still smoldering. She knew she was in the basement for sure though. The memory of being tossed down the rickety wooden steps was fresh in her mind; it was the events leading up to it that were fuzzy.

She was wet too and not from the basement, either. The cold concrete floor was bone dry save for droplets shaken loose from Beth when she landed. The cold, uncomfortable clinging of a wet t-shirt against her skin roused her enough to begin the process of clearing a path through her mind that would allow her memory to jog.

None of what was happening seemed real, so it was hard to differentiate reality from her over-active imagination. If she focused hard enough she could glimpse flashes of memories before the pain in her head closed off access to them. Regardless of being temporarily incapacitated at the bottom of the basement steps, Beth was still trapped.

She remembered seeing her aunt enter the living room dripping wet, her visage contorted into a hideously impossible version of evil. Beth remembered her aunt's words as clearly as she remembered the exaggeratedly pointed teeth protruding awkwardly from the mouth they were delivered from. That was what spurred Beth to her feet—the words, not the grotesque maw.

We're going to kill you.

There was a flippancy to the way she said it, a nonchalance that likened killing Beth to just another day at the office, which appeared to be the case. She backed toward the front door, looking from her aunt to her mother while waiting for the punch line that would make this bad joke worth it. Beth pleaded for help with her eyes each time she looked to her mother but was met with only an apathetic shrug accompanied by a devilish smirk.

Whatever was happening to Beth, it was clear she had no allies amongst the two women across the room from her. Aunt Agnes took a step forward, and her soaking dress sloshed with the movement, sending ripples through the puddle widening around her.

Beth detected movement from the corner of her eye and turned to see her mother had stood up from the couch, arms folded and clearly annoyed.

"Honestly, there's nothing you can do about it," her mother said.

"You're going to die, and we're going to kill you."

Beth watched her mother's eyes change to the same shade of yellow Aunt Agnes's eyes were. If she hadn't watched it happen she would've assumed her mother had popped in a pair of novelty contact lenses from the Halloween store. The real thing was far more menacing than any contact lenses could make them look, and this was no Halloween prank.

Beth whirled around on her heel and snatched the doorknob, turning and pulling at the same time. She was prepared to dash out into the encroaching trees to take her chances trying to escape through the forest. Unfortunately, this was no longer an option. The trees were right up against the house now, having ripped through the porch. Their trunks were touching the doorframe.

The trees had crowded closer together during their migration, leaving only inches between them, making escape through the front door impossible. Beth's eyes shot over in the direction of the living room window, but long, dark shadows behind the glass told her she wasn't going to be able to get out that way, either.

A cold breeze whistled through the narrow gaps in the trees, and the temperature in the house dropped another few degrees, adding a bite to the already uncomfortable chill. She slammed the door and whirled back around, but before it smacked the frame she heard the fevered squawks of what must have been dozens of blackbirds.

"Beth." Her mother's complexion had darkened into a zigzagging cluster of deep-red scars. "Honey, there's nowhere to go, but to be honest, there never was. This has always been your only purpose."

Beth felt her body temperature rise, burning off the fear so anger could fill the space. The lump in her throat was gone. Her teeth clenched, released, then clenched again, and her fingers curled into fists so tight her nails pierced the soft skin of her palms.

"I hope you're not arrogant enough to assume you're the first *daughter* we've used in The Cycle?" Aunt Agnes said.

Aunt Agnes's voice grew raspier with each word she pushed past the razors jutting from her gums. It sounded like she was actively scraping her vocal cords with the fine side of a cheese grater so as to prolong the use, but not quality of her voice.

"This *is* the entire reason you were born," her mother chimed in, trying to distract from the harshness of her sister's remark.

Her voice had taken on a deeper, gruffer quality as well, but not to the extreme of what Aunt Agnes's voice had devolved into. The burns on Beth's mother's face, while disfiguring, weren't as bad as the twisted horror show her aunt's had become.

"No," Beth spat defiantly. "No, this is all wrong. What you're saying is wrong!"

Aunt Agnes took another waterlogged step forward. Her dress sloshed from being pushed far past the saturation point. Beth caught a glimpse of light coming from the kitchen down the hall behind the lumbering, wet woman. While escaping out the front was no longer an option there was a small chance she could get out through the back door.

If the trees hadn't made it all the way up to that side of the house yet she could slip out and attempt to navigate the sentient forest, but first she had to make it past Aunt Agnes. Without wasting another second thinking about it Beth charged forward.

She didn't want to truly have a physical confrontation with this terrifying version of her aunt and hoped to avoid contact altogether. Her mother would be no threat from where she stood by the couch, making it impossible for her to head Beth off at the pass. Once she hit the hallway she'd be home free, so to speak, but she had to get there first.

Beth never played any organized sports growing up, but a vague interest kept them in her periphery since she was a child. She was pretty sure it sprung from having seen The Harlem Globetrotters appear on *Scooby-Doo*. She'd also seen highlight footage of professional running backs change direction on a dime to elude defenders.

She'd never performed one of these particular 'moves' but understood the mechanics of the motion, confident she could imitate it. No better options came to mind in the fraction of a second Beth had to make a decision, and she was already shifting the positioning of her shoulders to make it appear as if she were going to attempt to pass her aunt on the right.

In her mind Beth could see the maneuver being executed and did her best to replicate the motion she saw in her head with her body. She maintained contact with the jaundice-yellow eyes of her aunt, whose frightening smile grew grotesquely wider. She heard frantic scratching on the floor from behind as her mother raced to cut her off a beat too late, as predicted.

Beth mimed throwing her weight to the right when she got within a step of her aunt, planted her right foot, and cut quickly back left, hoping to pass the horrid woman without incident.

She heard the pop before she felt anything.

The first thing Beth felt was wet and cold from slamming into the chest of her sopping aunt who was not fooled by the poorly executed attempt to elude her. A moment later the pain exploded from Beth's knee and reverberated through her body, causing temporary blindness. She didn't know what happened to her knee, but she knew it wasn't good. This was the type of injury that required professional players to be taken off the field in a cart, but there was no cart coming for her.

She must have bounced off Aunt Agnes and ended up on the floor because when she could see again Beth found herself face down in the wetness the woman's dress perpetually excreted. She started to crawl on her stomach toward the hall, arms her only working form of propulsion.

Her knee screamed its catastrophic distress signal on loop as she dragged the useless leg along behind. Beth screamed in defiance against the pain as she desperately heaved herself forward, but the wet wood made it difficult for her palms to find enough purchase to move as fast as she wanted.

The women didn't snatch Beth up right away, which would have been quite easy for either or both to do. Beth refused to look back, but she knew her mother and aunt were toying with her. They were letting her struggle down the hall just far enough for her to know there truly was no escape, and as soon as she did the women grabbed her by the ankles.

She only caught a glimpse before she was yanked back, but it was enough to very clearly see the trees were touching the glass on both the window above the sink and on the back door. Cracks spider webbed in, jagged-lined circles where the trees touched the glass, and the backdoor was ever so slightly bowed in with a splintery crack running vertically where it would soon split apart from the tree's aggressive encroachment.

The pain in her knee momentarily blotted blackness across her mind, and she suddenly found herself slung over Aunt Agnes's shoulder. She lifted her head and saw her mother following close behind, leering with hard-set, compassionless, yellow eyes.

"I do hate it when they struggle, Agnes," Beth's mother said as she caught up. "Can't you do something about it?"

"Don't ask me," Agnes huffed the words in a way that implied she didn't care more than she didn't know. "This one was yours."

This one was yours?

Aunt Agnes flung the basement door open, and a rush of cold, rotten smelling, stale air blew up the steps. The smell was pungent enough to rouse Beth to alertness a moment before she was tossed down into the gaping darkness like a bag of dirty laundry being thrown to the wash.

The words *this one was yours* repeated in her head until she hit the cold cement floor where unconsciousness wrapped its filthy black hands around her mind.

NINETEEN

BETH'S MOTHER'S NAME WAS BEATRIX. She and her sister, Agnes, were far older than they appeared or anyone would ever guess them to be. With the power the two wielded they could make themselves look any age they wanted and only donned their true form for affect when it served a purpose.

Beth had correctly heard the word *witch* when her mother was speaking but knew nothing of the 'how' and 'why' surrounding it. Beatrix and Agnes were indeed witches but ancient witches who'd survived hundreds of years since their initial persecution during the witch-hunts and trials of the 1690s. The sisters even managed to survive being executed, although they were left with eternal reminders of the attempt.

They were able to achieve this feat because of The Cycle and their allegiance to Lilith, demon Princess of Hell. Their devotion and servitude were such to an extent the royal demon granted Beatrix and Agnes access to dark magic hidden in unknown pockets of Hell. Other witches had no way of gaining access to the places this power had been secreted away, nor were most of them even aware it existed.

In order to build the armies of Hell Lilith would steal the seed of men to impregnate herself with another demon for Legion, and she'd recruited the sisters to aid her cause. Using enchanted seduction they would lure men out to the forest for sex where they would then invoke Lilith, who took what she required of the poor, terrified bastard. Afterward the sisters were free to do what they wished with the man, which was always to kill him on the spot.

They would harvest his blood and organs to use in various potions and rituals as needed, and as a bonus, it pleased Lilith greatly to see the women rip the man apart with their bare hands. On the rare occasion they kept a man alive it was only for a short amount of time when they needed to extract pure adrenaline from the gland in his brain. This was a potent ingredient called for in only the most dangerous of spells.

While other witches and covens were being hunted down and killed after being given a so-called 'trial,' Beatrix and Agnes were able to repel hunters using the powers granted them by Lilith. Some years before witch-hunting was at its height the sisters took in a young girl who had wandered out of the woods, confused and scared.

The girl didn't know who she was or how she'd come to be walking in the woods and was on the brink of starvation. Instead of descending upon the girl and tearing her apart for her blood, they decided to nurse her to health and raise the girl as if she were a daughter to both of them. They called her Fawn because she reminded them of a newborn baby deer when she'd stumbled out of the forest.

They taught Fawn the ways of Lilith and magic but were careful not to let the young girl learn too much lest she one day try to turn on the sisters. The witches even used a special enchantment on the girl that would erase her memory of everything they taught her if invoked. The sisters trusted no one, which was the primary reason they'd survived as long as they had.

One night Agnes had a vision of she and Beatrix being caught by the hunters and killed by fire and drowning. After seeing the ghastly scene of her own horrific death, Lilith showed her something else. It was The Cycle, and if the sisters completed it they would not die from what the hunters were going to do to them.

She whispered in Agnes's ear that if they were to complete The Cycle every twenty-three years the sister-witches would continue to live on and on, never to feel the cold kiss of death. When Agnes came to she rushed out to the garden and told Beatrix they were going to have to kill Fawn.

Under the guise of showing the girl a 'sacred' ceremony, the sister witches brought Fawn to a space in the forest where they brought the men for Lilith. The fire burning in the center of the clearing was intense and raging, the flames having been stoked by magic.

Agnes and Beatrix flanked Fawn, each taking one of the girl's hands as they led her up to the fire. The heat pulsed around the women, baking them until Agnes snapped her fingers, casting a spell to shield them from the extreme temperature.

"What are we—?" Fawn started but quickly shut her mouth when Beatrix brought a finger to her lips and glared.

The sisters began reciting an incantation under their breath in a language Fawn was unfamiliar with. They increased the pace of their chant, and Fawn was suddenly able to feel heat from the fire again. She pulled back, but the sisters held her firmly in place. The girl screamed as the steadily scorching heat raised blisters on her face and arms that tore open into hundreds of weeping gashes.

The witches held her in place despite the desperate flailing and shrieking while they continued the incantation faster and louder.

Fawn's face started to blacken, and fluid from holes in her seared skin leaked thick, viscous pus that evaporated slowly despite the heat.

The chanting stopped as abruptly as it began, and for a moment Fawn felt frozen in time, no longer able to feel heat or the pain it caused. She couldn't feel the ground beneath her bare feet anymore either, but that's because she was hovering five inches above it. Agnes and Beatrix still held Fawn's hands in their gnarled death-grip as they recited the final words.

"Birth," Agnes said loudly over the roar of the flames, raising her other hand into the air.

"Restoration," said Beatrix, mimicking her sister's volume and motion.

"Power."

The witches said the last word in unison and for a moment everything stopped. The flames froze in place, taking on the appearance of fire captured forever in a lifelike oil painting. The air around the women stopped as well, giving Fawn a brief respite from the heat, but the moment was over before she felt it happen.

She didn't realize she was falling into the fire until her face smacked against one of the burning logs. The flames surged around her body and consumed her whole, both inside and out. Her eyeballs burst right away, but she wouldn't have been able to see the charred flesh on her thigh slide down off the bone or the skin dripping from her forearms anyway. Pain turned into continuous pressure that built and built until it was abruptly released and Fawn didn't feel anything anymore.

Agnes and Beatrix remained at the edge of the fire, still protected by the spell, and watched the girl they'd been raising as a daughter turn into a black, unrecognizable lump of death. The flames raged higher and the form of Lilith rose from the tips like smoke.

The demon Princess looked down upon the witches, a smoky-spectral smile upon her face.

The flames jumped again, engulfing the image, and when they receded a blackbird flew from the center of the fire and perched on a small branch hanging from the tallest tree. The bird paused a moment to regard the women below before releasing a piercing squawk that echoed through the forest as it leapt from the branch and disappeared off into the woods.

Without Fawn between them, Agnes and Beatrix now held each other's hand. The sisters turned from the fire, walked through the clearing, and through the woods back to their home, holding hands the entire time. When they got there they sat and waited for the hunters they already knew were coming to get them.

The Cycle was complete, but it didn't spare the women from being captured or burned at the stake or drowned with stones holding them beneath the water. What it did spare them from was dying, and by the time the party of witch hunters realized the tried and true methods of dispatching their prey weren't working, it was too late.

The sisters emerged, disfigured and hideous, and used the new power given them by Lilith to pop the arms and legs from each hunter with a wave of their hand. Agnes and Beatrix returned home, feeling neither pain nor discomfort from their injuries. They were unable to use Lilith's magic to permanently restore their burned and broken bodies as the demon wanted it to serve as a constant reminder of what they would be without her.

The witches were able to use enchantments that disguised their appearance, which they changed each Cycle, but their true form would always remain as it was after their time with the hunters.

Every twenty-three years another Cycle had to be performed if the sisters expected to keep living, but now it wouldn't be as simple as finding a girl, gaining her trust, and sacrificing her. For The Cycle to continue, Lilith required a daughter born from one of the witches as her offering.

They fell in line without missing a beat, and Agnes was the first of the two to carry a child. They decided to trade the responsibility of birth back and forth every twenty-three years, taking turns at being a temporary parent to the child, but first she would need to be impregnated. Agnes used a spell to make her appear as a young, beautiful woman, and then walked through the forest to the nearest town.

It didn't take long for her to catch the eye of a young man who was the son of a stable owner. Agnes could feel his eyes burning into her back as she passed by and was able to sense his lust rise, enveloping all common sense and decency. The witch stopped, turned to the man, and stepped toward him with long, confident strides. Her eyes were locked onto his until she closed them before leaning in to kiss the man hard on the mouth.

They lingered in the kiss for a moment, and Agnes slid her tongue in and out of the man's mouth, circling his as it desperately spun to keep up. Agnes pulled away, clutched the left lapel of his jacket, and gently pulled him along with her. The man did not resist as she led him toward the path in the forest she'd entered through.

He tried to speak, but before he could get two syllables out, Agnes looked back at him with her finger against her lips, her head shaking ever so slightly. He complied, not wanting his unnecessary questioning to ruin this opportunity for him. When they reached the path Agnes led him by the shirt for a few more feet before suddenly pushing him off into some brush.

He landed on his back, and Agnes descended upon him, immediately ripping away his clothes to take what she came for. It didn't take long for Agnes to be fertilized by the stable owner's son, but before he had a chance to bask in the glow of his poor performance

Agnes removed the spell that concealed her true form.

He looked up at the folds of charred burn scars covering the face of the woman who was still on top of him. He couldn't make sense of what he was seeing. Gone was the beautiful and seductive stranger who'd led him into the woods for an afternoon tryst, and in her place was a burn-covered beast with oozing tears in her skin.

The remaining air in the man's lungs was forced out by his diaphragm for the purpose of screaming, but before the process was complete Agnes had reached down and ripped out his neck with a single bare hand. Now the only noise he could make was a light and gentle gurgling sound that would alert no one.

It was over for now, and Agnes knew she was pregnant because Lilith willed it so. Agnes stood up after she'd watched the life leave the man's eyes and greedily licked the blood from her hand.

She stepped over the never-to-be father's body back onto the path and headed to the home she shared with her sister. She was a little way down the path when she stopped, turned around, and walked back to the body. She wanted to take his eyes. You never knew when a good pair of eyes was going to come in handy. The ocular orbs slipped effortlessly from the man's skull as she plucked them gingerly between her thumb and forefinger before dropping them unceremoniously in a leather pouch hanging from her hip.

Every twenty-three years the sister-witches performed The Cycle, honoring Lilith and providing her with soldiers in Hell. In return, the two remained immortal and continued to cultivate and strengthen the powers bestowed upon them with each passing year. They constantly changed and adapted to fit the current time period and found they were able to hide in plain sight.

The fear of witches faded over the years until they had turned into imaginary characters with pointy hats riding around on broomsticks. The more time that passed, the easier it was for the sisters to operate until they managed to blend in so well they were completely undetectable. As long as they performed the ceremony of The Cycle every twenty-three years they would continue this way forever.

TWENTY

BETH FLUTTERED IN AND OUT of consciousness while lying at the bottom of the basement steps. From one moment to the next she felt either the five-alarm fire of pain that consumed her entire body, or she felt nothing at all. Finally, she went out and stayed out.

She dreamt she was driving her Jeep on one of the roads that ran around the mountain. The windows were down and the song "Hole in the Sky" from Black Sabbath's *Sabotage* album was blasting from the speakers. Beth's hair whipped in the cool rush of air like streamers on the handle of a child's bicycle, and she felt happy, she felt free.

There was a hint of smoke in the air—no doubt from a nearby campfire or barbecue pit—but the smell grew stronger and was no longer pleasant. She couldn't put her finger on it exactly but thought it might be burning plastic or maybe rubber? Beth scrunched her nose, trying to reject the smell from advancing farther up her nostrils, and glanced up in the rearview mirror.

The backseat was on fire. The rubber and plastic she smelled burning was coming from the melting lump the bench seat was rapidly becoming. She looked back to the road just in time to watch it drop out from beneath her. She fell for what felt like forever as fire continued to lay claim to the vehicle while Beth retained her grip on the useless steering wheel. As the flames began melting the driver seat around Beth, the Jeep hit the water.

She opened her eyes, sat up, and coughed out the liquid she was choking on. She wasn't in the Jeep or the ocean but still on the basement floor. Her aunt and mother stood over her. An empty, wet bucket dangled from Agnes's hand. The pain shrieking from her knee brought Beth all the way back and pushed out any lingering memory of the nightmare.

She didn't need to remember details to know there wasn't much difference between the awful dream and her frightful reality. She looked up at the women smiling down on her bruised and broken body. The witches must have felt they'd made their point by showing Beth their fire-mangled forms because they'd changed back to what she was accustomed to seeing.

The burns had been smoothed out into soft, youthful-looking skin, and as far as Beth could tell, Aunt Agnes was bone dry. She looked from the face of a woman she'd only met once to one she'd known her entire life and realized she didn't actually know either of them.

Beth grappled with the notion that the woman who birthed her, raised her, and been there every step of the way was about to kill her without a modicum of compunction. Despite their familiar forms and modified features Beth could see the evil behind their eyes telegraphing their murderous intentions quite clearly. There was no mistake, and Beth knew it. These women *were* going to kill her.

"Time to wake up, darling," her mother said as Agnes splashed the small amount of water still clinging to the bottom and sides of the bucket into Beth's face.

She blinked the water from her eyes as they adjusted to the darkness of the basement. She could see tiny flames dancing wickedly atop candles perched at various heights behind the witches. As far as Beth could tell, the candles were the sole source of light in the entire basement, and the way they backlit the sisters added a sinister element to their already dominating presence.

"Come now, Beth," Aunt Agnes said, leaning over, offering the girl her hand.

Beth tried to push herself up, but her knee reminded her a powder keg of pain was ready to blow at the slightest wrong movement. A meek yelp inadvertently leapt from Beth's lips, and she gritted her teeth, instantly regretting showing yet another sign of weakness.

She begrudgingly reached out to take her Aunt's hand but balked and pulled back suddenly, as if her fingers had accidently grazed a hot stovetop. She didn't want any help from this woman.

"I told you," Agnes said to her sister. "If you would have let me take her when I tried this would be a lot easier."

She was referring to the time she'd come to the park, apparently hoping to retrieve the girl.

"Okay, okay," grumbled Beatrix. "Next time we do it your way."

Agnes preferred to raise the sacrifices as they had Fawn. She felt the girls were easier to manipulate toward the end because they trusted the witches right up until the point they realized not to, but by then it was too late. Plus, the women benefitted from having what equated to a live-in servant for twenty-three years.

When Beatrix birthed she preferred to keep her sacrifices in the dark, letting them believe they're living a normal life until tricking them out to the house where the sisters derived much pleasure toying with them like they'd done with Beth. Unlike Agnes, Beatrix wanted to prolong the suffering of her birthed sacrifice.

Agnes grunted in frustration as she tossed the bucket aside and reached down to grab Beth under each arm. The pain-bomb in her knee threatened to detonate as she was aggressively lifted to her feet, but Beth bit back every urge to scream.

She stood shakily, putting as little weight as possible on her right leg. She couldn't imagine the pain in her knee getting any worse, or didn't want to, at least. Doing her best to maintain balance, Beth noticed a new pain shouting to make its presence known on her right side. She'd most likely cracked or broken some ribs in the fall, and the sudden change in her position exacerbated the injury.

"We know you're scared and confused," her mother said, taking a step closer to her daughter. "Soon it will all be over and pain will never exist for you again in this realm."

The witch reached out to caress the side of Beth's face as if the mother-daughter bond they shared hadn't been maligned by magic, murder, and demons over the last few hours. She struggled to step back away from her mother and bumped against the wall behind her, but there hadn't been a wall behind her. She slid her hands from the sides of her thighs back to touch it, and she immediately knew it wasn't the basement wall she'd backed into. It was a tree.

Beth looked to the stairs she'd been thrown down, but trees stood in place of them, as well. She looked past her mother and saw the familiar tall, dark trees grouped too close together to allow room for escape. They had encircled the three women like in Beth's dreams.

The flames flickering behind her mother and aunt weren't bouncing from the wick of a candle but were suspended in the air, attached to nothing. Aunt Agnes waved her hand, and the small flames twisted and spun to the center of the clearing. They lingered, combining into one single flame that dove into the ground and exploded into a raging bonfire.

TWENTY-ONE

BETH NEVER KNEW HER FATHER but remained unaffected by his absence in her life. She never experienced a longing pang for that missing aspect in her upbringing described to her by friends with absentee fathers. Some were angry with the men who'd walked out of their lives, regardless of lacking the capacity with which to understand the complexities of a relationship, let alone a marriage.

The ones who weren't angry were sad but confused about why. When Beth would enquire as to why they were sad or what about the situation made them feel sad, none of her fellow father-less chums could express it. Some would shrug and say it was because their mommy was sad. Others said their mommies *told* them to be sad, tricking the child into commiserating in her misery.

The one thing that set Beth apart from these kids was they all actually knew their fathers. They stayed with the estranged man every weekend, or at the very least, every other weekend. Some would even spend the summer with the person they weren't sure why they were supposed to hate. They would come back laden with clothes and toys and would be happy for a brief time before their mother's dourness seeped in to poison them all over again.

Beth had never seen a picture of her father or even known his name. She asked her mother about him once and was actually told the truth, or a version of the truth the young girl could handle.

Her mother said she honestly didn't know much about the man to tell. She very plainly told her daughter she'd had a short fling with a man who was long gone before she knew she was pregnant. She didn't even remember his name. Her mother told Beth without a patronizing sugarcoating that as a young woman she'd made some mistakes and wasn't as careful as she should have been with her sexual partners.

She told Beth finding out she was pregnant was what helped her to straighten her life out, and she had no regrets. She said if given the chance she would've made the same decision a hundred more times over because of how much Beth meant to her. Beth was the most important person in her world, and she wouldn't be able to live without her cherished daughter.

Beth had no idea the amount of truth there was in that statement. Never in her wildest dreams could she have fathomed what it truly meant or the weight the words held. She was satisfied with her mother's answer despite its bluntness. Beth loved and trusted her mother, and as far as she knew, these feelings were reciprocated. She had no idea she was born to die and serve eternally in hell without getting the chance to have an actual reason to go there.

Beth's father wasn't a one-night stand who blew in and out of town like a summer thundershower. His name was Stephen Wiseman, but he went by Zipp Ripper. He was a musician who sang in a horror-metal band called The Rippers, hence the pseudonym. His sharp features and abundance of tattoos gave him a striking look that helped sell the image he portrayed.

The Rippers were a midlevel act known more for their onstage horror show than any of their actual songs. Still, the band managed to pick up one small, shitty tour after another and put the pieces together the best they could. They made enough money to get to the next show, put a meal in their bellies, and buy whatever drugs and booze they could get with what they had left.

Some nights were cocaine and top-shelf whiskey while others were cheap beer and trucker-speed. It wasn't the best life, but it was good enough for Zipp, plus it had been working all this time, so why change anything?

It happened on the second to last night of what would be The Rippers last tour. The rest of the band didn't remember much of the night and were no help to police, who wrote them off as drunks and drug addicts.

They remembered birds perched over the door of the bar they loaded their equipment through. Blackbirds. They remembered a girl standing close to the stage. They all remarked on how attractive she was but for the life of them could not describe her face.

They remembered seeing Zipp being led down a hallway after the show by that same girl. They saw her duck into a door on the right side of the hall and pull Zipp in with her. They remembered drinking something, smoking something, snorting something, but they didn't remember much of anything else until they woke up in the van parked outside the bar where they'd left it. The massive hangovers that accompanied the band members being conscious didn't help to jog their memory any, either.

The police led the other four members of The Rippers down the hall and into the room Zipp and the mystery girl disappeared into in hopes the gruesome scene would help them recall the forgotten details of the prior evening. Upon entering the room, three of The Rippers with already shaky stomachs expelled their boozy contents down onto their ratty Chuck Taylors, which were no stranger to being vomited on.

The fourth Ripper, the drummer known as T-Top, managed to step back into the hallway before jettisoning the foul concoction of liquor and mystery chunks from his stomach. When there was nothing left, T-Top sat down hard next to the puddle of his sick, leaned back against the wall, and started to bawl. He did not want to go back into that room again.

While the scene was especially grisly and violent, the officers were surprised a group of men who sang songs primarily about death and made themselves up to perpetually look like the walking dead fell to pieces when faced with the personification of their brand in reality. Two of the deputies shared a look and chuckle that went unnoticed by the shaken Rippers.

From the waist up Zipp was still wearing the sleeveless black t-shirt with an interpretation of the Grim Reaper screened onto the front of it. His jeans were pulled down to his ankles, and his shoes were still on. What made this scene particularly unsettling was that the top and bottom halves of Zipp were no longer connected. The torso was propped up on a leather couch against the wall directly across from the door while the singer's lower half lay in a heap off in the far left corner of the room.

A trail of blood, viscera, and bodily fluid led from the couch to the corner where the lower section of his body had been dragged. Pieces of intestine and chunks of flesh and muscle dotted the path like a morbid post-modern art instillation.

His testicles, which were found on the couch next to his torso, were now shriveled, black lumps. They had been so badly burned they couldn't be identified until the coroner performed an autopsy. They had been exposed to an extreme heat that fused them together into one solid piece, but nothing else in the room had been burned. There weren't even any scorch marks left beneath or around the lump to indicate it had ever even been hot.

The entire room was void of fingerprints, DNA, and any other clues as to the offender's identity. The only witnesses were too fried to remember anything about the woman Zipp disappeared with despite all having remarked on her attractiveness. The bartenders and other staff working that night were questioned thoroughly, but not a single one had witnessed anything out of the ordinary.

When asked about the girl Zipp was partying with after the show, they claimed not to know what the investigators were talking about. They remembered seeing him partying and drinking with the rest of the band at the bar, and then he just wasn't with them anymore. None of them saw Zipp with a girl.

Despite the brutality of the attack and how messy it was the police had no evidence to go on. Not a single trace of the killer could be found in the entire crime scene. In the end it was determined whomever killed Zipp had a personal vendetta against him and had used professionals to take him out. That was that. The case was filed away, and they were on to the next one.

Only one person knew what really happened to Zipp in that room, and it was Beth's mother, Beatrix. She'd made herself look like the young, pretty goth girls who typically attended a show by The Rippers. The spell she used not only disguised her true form, but also made it impossible for anyone who saw her to be able to describe what she looked like.

Catching Zipp's attention was easy and required little effort on Beatrix's part. When she had him alone the sex was quick, passionless, and utilitarian. It was over quickly, and having got what she came for, the witch invoked the power of Lilith and tore the singer in half. The last thing Zipp saw were his testicles burning in her hand.

Nine months later Beatrix would give birth to the next sacrifice, and The Cycle would continue. Beth would never know who her father was or how much like him she'd grown to become.

TWENTY-TWO

BETH'S MIND RACED AS SHE scanned the circle of trees looking for any possible opening she could squeeze through. No longer was she struggling to accept what was happening to her and was now only concerned with survival. She was so consumed with finding a way out she didn't notice the way her mother was looking at her.

Beatrix typically never thought about or even remembered the men she'd used throughout the years to complete The Cycle, but the way the fire light hit Beth's face, accentuating the sharpness of her chin, nose, and cheekbones, stirred a memory. She couldn't recall a name or the surrounding circumstances, but she did remember a face, the face of Beth's father.

The way Beth held her head with her chin tilted up and slightly cocked to one side mimicked the cool confidence the long dead musician exuded on stage. The way her mouth was slightly parted, her lower lip trembling, and how her eyes watered but refused to spill a tear matched the face he'd made when he realized he was in trouble that night. Unfortunately for him, this realization came after Beatrix had ripped him in half.

The memory stirred the witch's bloodlust, and she grew impatient for the start of the ceremony, the completion of The Cycle. Beatrix was incensed at the gall of her daughter to even inadvertently remind her of the man she was forced to couple with for the survival of her and Agnes. She wished for a moment she could go back in time to tear the naïve fool apart all over again, but killing Beth would serve her need just the same.

Destroying the girl would be like killing her father again while putting a permanent end to the last thing he was linked to. Killing the man was one thing, but ending his lineage was a completely different kind of satisfaction.

The familiar screeching of the blackbird sounded from across the circle. The shaking of a lower limb drew Beatrix's eyes to where the bird had landed, and it cried out again when Beth made eye contact with it. The blackbird was alone, or at least that's what Beth thought, but quickly realized she'd been mistaken. In the darkness of the forest behind the bird Beth saw dozens of tiny black orbs glowing red around the rim.

The blackbirds were here and so was Lilith.

Beatrix stepped toward her daughter with her hands out, but Beth began limping around the circle, keeping her back against the trees. Her mother remained directly in front of her despite Beth's awkward shuffling, and she glanced down to see the ground was moving beneath her feet like she was walking sideways on a treadmill. No matter how many steps she took Beth stayed in the same place, exactly where the sister witches wanted her.

"Darling, while I admire your spirit," her mother started as she took another step, "you should realize by now there is no way out of this. Your conception and birth were for this sole purpose."

Aunt Agnes stopped chanting and turned from the fire to join her sister.

"You've always belonged to Lilith," Aunt Agnes said. "We're sending you home."

The blackbirds began to squawk and rustle their wings, creating a nightmarish soundscape that swirled around the small clearing, coating everything it touched in a sticky film of darkness. When the blackbirds settled, the sound spun up and over the trees where it decayed quickly in the open air. Beatrix and Agnes, having taken advantage of the distraction, stepped up to Beth. Her mother clutched Beth's right hand and Aunt Agnes took the left.

All at once it was silent and still, like the air had become too thick to hear through and so heavy it pinned everything in place lest the slightest motion pierce the suffocating veil. Beth could feel an unnatural heat pulsing from her mother and Aunt's hand, but it did not burn her.

The pressure in the clearing changed drastically, causing Beth's ears to pop and begin ringing immediately after. She reflexively jerked her hands up to cover them, but the witches held them firm at her sides. She managed a glance over at her mother, who was looking into the fire and smiling, then over at her aunt, who was doing the same. Then Beth saw it too, although she wished she hadn't.

Hovering in the flames was a translucent female figure she couldn't help but stare at. The presence demanded her attention and refused to relinquish control, but Beth wasn't fighting it anymore. The figure's long hair was made of black flames that floated and flickered around the ghostly form. Her eyes were the color of death, and her smile was dark and lovely.

Despite striking a terrifying figure, Beth was not afraid and, in fact, found herself enamored with the being. The woman holding Beth's hand wasn't really her mother, and she understood that now. Lilith was her mother, and she was calling Beth home to the fire.

She thought she was floating until Beth realized the pain in her knee and feet was gone, and she was able to walk with ease. The fire roared as the three women approached it hand in hand, but Aunt Agnes's enchantment deflected its intense heat. The only warmth Beth felt was what radiated from the witch's palms, and the sensation worked to comfort her.

The fiery form hovered in the flames and cast her obsidian gaze down upon the next daughter to join her army in Hell. Agnes and Beatrix started chanting in a language Beth had never heard before but could somehow understand.

Agnes lifted the protection from Beth and searing heat worked quickly to fill the available space around her. Her skin grew red and ruptured in places across her body, but Beth couldn't feel anything. The flesh on her fingers and hands burned off quick, like fog under the glaring morning sun, and the muscle beneath melted and oozed slowly from the bones.

Beth's mother and aunt slipped their hands away, dragging with them strands of drippy flesh that fell slowly to the forest floor like cheese from a piping-hot slice. She was no longer being held in place, but Beth didn't try to run. She didn't want to anymore.

She could see it now. She could feel it. Everything the witches told her was true. Beth was born for one purpose, and she was in the midst of fulfilling it. She'd never felt anything as satisfying in her life, and it was taking death to experience it. Beth could see the reflection of herself burning in the impossible blackness of Lilith's eyes, and smiled.

The cartilage from her ears filled and covered the canals into her head, so she was no longer able to hear what the witches behind her were saying. But if she could, she'd be hearing her mother say *Birth* followed by her aunt saying *Restoration*.

As the sisters sung the word *Power* in unison Beth stepped into

Lilith's fiery embrace and let it consume her. The blackbirds' flapping wings mimicked the sound of a thousand rattlesnakes as the creatures swooped into the clearing before flying up and over the trees to disappear against a starless sky.

As the sound of the birds' retreat decayed, the fire, which no longer contained Beth or Lilith, waned along with it until there was only silence and darkness.

TWENTY-THREE

THE BASEMENT DOOR SWUNG OPEN and Beatrix entered the kitchen holding a handmade basket containing five medium-sized jars, three with screw-on lids and the others topped with a cork. She kicked the door shut behind her and called out to her sister.

"Agnes? Agnes, you told me you were going to help me with this."

Beatrix now appeared as a younger, but modern, version of herself. Her straight, black hair dangled above bare shoulders, exposed as a result of the sleeves being cut from the t-shirt she wore. The shorts she had on were also cut, the bottom of her pockets peaking out from behind frayed denim.

She walked the basket across the kitchen, placed it on the counter next to the sink, and took the jars out one by one. Beatrix moved the empty basket to the other side of the sink and spaced the jars out evenly on the counter in front of her. The upper portion of her left arm was tattooed from shoulder to elbow with a photo-realistic image of a blackbird. The detail in the piece was stunning, the linework sharp and clear.

119

It was the product of a professional's hand, made steady and confident from thousands of hours of practice, or at least that's the look she was going for. A needle never touched the witch's skin to deliver the indelible design but was instead conjured from a picture in her mind.

"Agnes," she called to her sister again with annoyance invading her tone. "I can't put this together without you. Now get your ass in here!"

Agnes was sitting at the desk in her study, typing into a sleek, silver laptop. The modern device was absurdly out of place in the room and created a confusing clash against the surrounding aesthetic. It looked like the thing had been accidently left in the past by an irresponsible time traveler.

"I'll be right there, dear," she sang over her shoulder. "I'm just finishing up in here."

The witch's long, charred, bony fingers tapped at the keys with steady precision, each strike sounding a decisive and satisfyingly loud click. The room was dark but the dull glow from the screen was enough to illuminate the hideous features of her burned and bloated face. A small, black puddle was growing under her chair from the steady drip off the hem of her dress, and she absently tapped her foot in the water to the beat of a song playing in her head.

Agnes had two tabs open on her Internet browser, and she clicked back and forth between them, pausing occasionally to type. One of them was open to an email account she'd opened under the pseudonym Melissa Branford, and the other was open to a website called *Missed Connections*. This and other iterations of the site provided a forum for people who saw another person out in a public place they would like to meet but are either too busy or too scared to initiate communication in the moment.

The majority of the posts on any local version of the site were from men and read like the sad, white knight, posturing word vomit a secretly self-aggrandizing cuck-boy would write. These men didn't expect to hear back from anyone, which was what made it safe to spin a trite, backhanded soliloquy as a virtue-signal of the delicate sensibility they wished to project.

Agnes was using the website to select Lilith's donor on the years it was her turn to birth the sacrifice since she discovered it existed. Seducing these men was quick, easy, and required little to no enchantment on her part. Agnes felt she was doing all women a service by killing one of these men every twenty-three years. She was culling the weak from the herd.

She clicked from her email back over to the site to make sure she'd gleaned every morsel of information the post had to offer.

I saw you at my coffee shop last Friday. You were going out as I was going in, and I held the door for you. You smiled and my heart was instantly made a captive of your pearly-white prison. I was too stunned to speak and could only watch you walk away before disappearing around the corner. I've been back every morning for the last four days but haven't seen you since. Your chestnut colored hair, light green eyes, and precious upturned nose have haunted my dreams since that day prompting me to question whether or not you were just a dream. If you truly exist in the waking world please contact me. I'd love to have another chance to hold the door open for you.

Agnes clicked back over to her email, hit send, and, in the time it took to push the button, her appearance changed dramatically. Gone were the cracked, weeping burn scars and puffy, waterlogged flesh, replaced now with smooth, tight, young skin. In place of the dripping dress was a short but casual black miniskirt and a low-cut, matching blouse.

She tossed her head back and shook out the thick, slightly curled, chestnut-colored hair as it sprung from her scalp. Agnes didn't have to look exactly like the woman the man had seen because there was no woman, but her eyes turned to a light shade of green and her new nose curled up ever so slightly at the tip.

A soft chime rang from the laptop's tiny speakers, announcing a reply back from the message she'd just sent. She didn't open the email because she already knew what it said and instead opened the computer's camera.

The man was, of course, asking for a picture. They all asked for a picture. They wanted to be able to gaze upon the woman who bought the sappy, bland prose they baited their hook with.

They all asked for a photo on the grounds of *I need to know it's really you.* All they *needed* to know is if you were fuckable by their standards, and if so, they were all too eager to play the part of the stunned, love-struck jerkoff they made themselves out to be. When the man determined the woman had reached her expiration date, the veil was lifted, and the stranger retreated in order to continue preying on the vulnerable with a sociopathic nonchalance.

Agnes's new visage appeared on the screen in the window of the camera application, and she smiled at the tiny lens hole built into the top of the monitor. She tapped the spacebar and the speakers sounded a faux camera snap. The witch didn't bother to look at the photo. She didn't have to in order to know it was absolutely what the thirsty man on the other side wanted to see.

She attached the photo to her reply and a moment later he sent back an enthusiastic response. He gushed on about how he couldn't believe it was her and how he never does things like this and how it must be meant to be. He said they should meet up, but of course not at the coffee shop he claimed to have first saw her. His story could unravel too easily there, so he suggested they get a drink somewhere else.

He gave her the address of a local bar, but she already knew where it was. It was the same bar they always asked to meet her in, and Agnes knew it well. She replied, saying she would see him there tonight at eight and that she was very excited to meet him, adding an *xoxo* at the end.

She closed the laptop and smiled. The Cycle would continue and Lilith's legion would continue to grow. She got up from the chair, feeling much lighter on her feet in the new form she'd taken. Her journals were neatly organized against the back of the desk behind the laptop, and she noticed something peeking out from the top of one, pressed between the pages.

She reached over and pulled what turned out to be a black feather from the book. Agnes spun it by the stem between her thumb and finger for a moment before she tucked it behind her ear and skipped to the kitchen to help her sister.

Acknowledgments

Thanks to Carrie and Andy for always helping me keep it wet out there.

John Wayne Comunale lives in Houston, Texas to prepare himself for the heat in Hell. He writes weird horror and hosts the weekly storytelling podcast *John Wayne Lied to You*. He also fronts the punk rock disaster, johnwayneisdead, and travels around the country slinging books while giving truly unique performances of the written word. John Wayne was an American actor who died in 1979.

Other Grindhouse Press Titles